BLOSSOMED

KNUCKLES

BLOSSOMED

Blossomed

First Edition

Paperback ISBN: 979-8-8229-1975-4
eBook ISBN: 979-8-8229-1976-1

CHAPTER 1

It began with a Ouija board. It all seemed so silly and harmless at the time. Abby had gone with her ex-wife and some other buddies to one of the oldest cemeteries around, late at night. A large tree limb had fallen at their feet after they'd taken a few steps forward. One buddy had dashed back to the car afterward and said that he'd wait there. Though they all laughed and made fun of him for that, he'd been the smart one. The group of friends went way into the back of the place with their candles, beers, and bad attitudes. Abby and her crew were always so extra about everything, see. So, of course, if there were tombstones there from the Civil War era, that's where they just had to use the Ouija board.

Looking back on this, Abby would call herself a real dumbass. Yet she was thankful to have made the mistake too. It caused so many horrors, true. It brought upon her so much suffering and heartbreak; and yet, through the trials it brought her a greater understanding of what was going on in the world. Abby lost her sanity, her wife, her joy, and even her credibility! But she found God. She found understanding. She even found an enemy who became a friend. This is the story of a girl who blossomed into a woman, one that inspired others to come together and get out of the flock of sheep.

Abby was born with the name of Abigail Ray. Yet she went by the name Abby. *Abigail* just sounded too colonial for her tastes. She had been an only child, so she never really got away with anything growing up. She was spoiled and much too sheltered as a kid. To her parents, though, and to plenty of other Southern Baptists, she was much too different. Abby was a multigenre-loving music listener who would be jamming out to the Spice Girls one moment and then bopping her head up and down to Apashe the next. Abby's love for women instead of men, though—that was the last straw when it came to being different.

Her mother found out by snooping around in Abby's room and reading through her daughter's journal while Abby was preparing a bubble bath. She and Abby's dad forced their daughter to go to a "pray the gay away" place called Adam and Eve. They paid some Baptist therapists to "fix" their daughter. These people talked to Abby in two different sessions. In the first session, they gave her a book to read over for the next session, and no—not the Bible. She read it over with her girlfriend at the time. The two laughed at it and read aloud the parts that they found the most ridiculous. Abby's mother heard them laughing about it, of course. Abby still lived with her folks at that point, see.

Abby's mother waited until her daughter's girlfriend had left and then began hounding her for poking fun at a book that was supposed to make her feel bad for being attracted to the same gender. Yet when Abby went back with her mother and mother's friend for the next appointment, the therapist spoke with Abby first. The pale, dark-haired woman did well to appear expressionless, heartless even. She asked for Abby's thoughts on the book. Abby was blunt and honest with her in her answer. "I found it far from true, really."

The woman asked, "How can you say that?"

Abby explained, "I like women the same way that you like men. I don't feel guilty about it like some of the people in this book claimed in their testaments. It's simple. I like women, but I still love God. I know that he will love me no matter who I like. I'm human, just like you. He made us all imperfect. I'm pretty sure he considers that. If God is love, then he loves me for being me."

The therapist had Abby step out of the office after that. She called the girl's mother in there. Abby waited for what felt to her like an eternity, until finally her mother came out sobbing. She motioned for her daughter to follow her out to the car without words. Tears had always been Abby's mother's defense mechanism. Even now, it is what she used to get her friend breathing fire at Abby. See, Abby quietly got into the back of the car as her mom's friend asked what was wrong. Carla was the name that

Abby's mom went by. Carla had this damsel-in-distress-type personality that she used to get through life, and she played it well even now as she cried out, "They said that they couldn't change my daughter!" She bawled dramatically as her buddy glanced in the back at Abby. The friend pulled out of the "pray the gay away" establishment and headed home.

After an awkward silence with no sound but Carla's crying, the friend said to Abby, "So, are you happy destroying your mother like this?"

Abby replied, "What are you talking about? I'm not doing anything but existing."

The woman argued, "You know that she doesn't want you to be gay," to which Abby argued back, "Believe it or not, I can't change that. I'm not going to be someone I'm not just because someone else wants me to."

The lady pulled the car over, put her hazards on, and told Abby, "Then get out of my car."

Abby retorted, "We aren't even home yet."

Her mother's friend gave Abby a bitter laugh. "Well, looks like you're walking."

Abby waited for her mother to take her side. That didn't happen. Abby shrugged, said, "Fine—I like walking," and got out of the car. She closed the door, watched the wretched woman drive off, and walked the rest of the way home.

Life got even harder after that. To the little lesbian, it felt like the Christians were the ones throwing all the stones. Abby had been on the drama team and the puppet team at her church. Yet, due to her mother, Carla, calling and crying to everyone she knew about her daughter turning out to be gay, the puppet and theater ministry at this church kicked her out of both clubs. The head of the groups told her that he just couldn't have one of his performers being gay and around children. The man compared lesbians to pedophiles, which sent Abby pushing away from churches and anything God related for many years.

She moved away from her parents and got away from Southern Baptists and their hypocrisy. Abby got to spread her wings for the first time ever. She had many fun moments, but plenty of bad ones too. She had a few girlfriends that didn't last, customer service jobs that barely paid her bills, and parties she barely remembered. She met her ex-wife in the party phase.

The girl's name was Cleo. She was in the army at this time, had beautiful green eyes, and utter studliness that made Abby weak in the knees in those days. She was loud, confident, and mischievous. She was sweet, fun, and loved animals like Abby did. Poor Abby fell hard. The two got serious together, and Cleo got Abby a sweet and feisty pit bull mix named Khandi when she was deployed to Kandahar, Afghanistan. This dog was Abby's pride and joy, yet she had to have Cleo keep her when they divorced because she needed to move back in with her mother, who had a dog that didn't get along with Khandi. Life is tragic.

Getting back to the Ouija board incident, though, that's what really started the adventure of a lifetime. After many parties, many camping trips, and a few incidents where Abby died for a few seconds, she had endured quite a young adulthood. A little over a decade of that was devoted to her ex-wife, Cleo. She was there with Abby when they went with some buddies into the old cemetery that night with their beers and Ouija board. They all sat together in a circle. Abby sat in the soft grass and pleasantly watched Cleo set up the board while Brin and Ron placed candles in a circle around the board itself.

Cleo lit the candles, and the group got started. It all seemed ludicrous to them. They made jokes, drank their beers, and smoked a little bud, and Ron even went over to a nearby tombstone and took a piss. They gathered in a circle after getting situated, sat around the board, and each of them placed a hand on the piece that the spirit supposedly moved around the letters to spell out its message. It's hard to know if a spirit is moving this piece, or if it's just one of your friends playing around. This was the case with Abby's bunch. Brin had called out, "Hello. Is there a spirit among us?" The piece moved to *yes*.

Abby murmured, "Ooh!" as the others chuckled.

Brin asked it, "Who are we speaking with?"

The marker moved from this letter to that, until it had spelled out the response: "Call me Charlie."

Cleo scoffed at Ron and said to him, "You're moving the marker!" But Ron shook his head and replied, "No, I'm not!" She looked at the rest of them in an accusing manner, yet they all stared back at her with looks of innocence.

Abby argued with her wife: "I don't think any of us are moving it, honey." Cleo had taken her hand off the marker in irritation.

Brin spoke up. "Come on, this is why we're here!"

Cleo sighed and placed her hand back on the marker with the rest of them. She said, "Fine. Let's just get this over with and roll a blunt." This was agreed to, and they continued their inquisition with the use of the Ouija board.

Brin called out, "Are you still with us, Charlie?"

The marker moved to "*yes.*

Cleo asked the question this time. "What do you want?"

The letters that the marker moved to spell out this time chilled them all to the bone, though they wouldn't show it. The response read: "One of you."

Brin asked the next question: "How did you die?"

They got the reply, "Don't worry about that."

Abby broke hands this time. She pulled her hand free from the others, stood up, and commented, "I'm done. Let's go smoke."

The others broke away too. As they all proceeded to blow out candles and put the board and marker away, they argued over which one of them had been moving the piece around. It was almost a hidden hope, disguised as a belief, that it had simply been a friend moving the piece, and not some creepy spirit named Charlie that wanted one of them. Ron was moaning and groaning, "It was getting good! I just think we could've gone on a little longer," to which Abby joked back, "What, were you having fun coming up with a ghostly story about Charlie?"

Ron retorted, "I wasn't moving the piece!"

Abby rolled her eyes and gave him a sarcastic "Mm-hmm," as they all proceeded to go back to the car, where their other buddy was still waiting after the tree limb had scared him out of participating.

Though the group made their jokes about the Ouija board and made fun of their other friend for freaking out over the tree limb falling at their feet as soon as they'd gotten inside the cemetery, the incident turned out to be much more real than any of them had intended. Charlie turned out to be an actual entity. Yet he was not the ghost that you assume is the only type you can bring out with a Ouija board. Charlie wasn't a ghost at all.

The peculiar things that began to happen after this night of drunken Ouija board fun started out looking like a typical haunting, true enough. Things would disappear and pop up somewhere else, after Cleo or Abby had already looked for them there. Their dog would randomly start growling up at the wall or ceiling, and when one of them would look at the spot that the dog's eyes were trained on...there would be absolutely nothing there. Charlie never messed with Ron or Brin, but he haunted the mess out of Abby and Cleo.

The creepiest incident, at first, was one night at their old home. It was late, and they had settled into bed for the night. They had a roommate who worked with them at this time, and she had a bedroom right next to Cleo and Abby's room. The walls were very thin, and one could hear a pin drop in the other room! Well, their roommate, Samantha, had gone in there to go to sleep too. But a little later, while Abby and Cleo were trying to sleep, they kept hearing this heavy, repetitive breathing, along with constant footsteps pacing back and forward. The sounds were coming from

Samantha's room. The couple's dog, Khandi, began growling and looking at the wall separating the two rooms. Cleo and Abby both sat up in bed and stared at each other in mixed confusion and agitation. A spooky voice was heard whispering something very fast in there too.

Cleo got up and whispered to Abby, "That doesn't sound like Samantha." Abby urged her wife to go and see what was going on in there. She herself was much too afraid to do so. Cleo agreed to and left their own room after grabbing her gun. The sounds all stopped. Abby could hear Cleo talking to Samantha, but when she came back into their room, she looked very unsettled.

Abby asked, "What's up?"

Cleo replied, "Samantha was asleep in her bed with her headphones in when I got in there. She didn't hear anything that we did."

Abby and Cleo moved the first chance they got, and they figured that it would stop the haunted shit. Yet things even started disappearing at their new home. Khandi would still randomly start growling at empty spots here and there. One night, Cleo woke up feeling like something had rushed through her. It had been cold and unsettling for the stud, and she'd woken Abby up to talk to her about it. After she ranted to her a little, Abby had gotten out of their bed to go to the bathroom. Then she noticed something on her side. She flicked their lamp on and gasped. "I'm bleeding," she muttered.

Cleo looked where Abby motioned to, and on the side of her left hip were three bloodied marks that looked like claws had dug in. They were too deep and broad to have been done by their dog, though. It was the Roman symbol for the mark of the beast! It's funny how something that unsettling can make an atheist like Abby's ex start believing in God, angels, and demons. See, the Charlie that they'd spoken to in that cemetery was a demon. He was one of the fallen angels themselves. That's why they were still being haunted even after moving houses.

Cleo had her sweet little Catholic grandmother come over the next day and bless their house. She stocked them up with sage, crosses, and holy water. Yet it barely helped. Charlie liked to haunt Abby the most. Her reactions entertained him so much. She was the overly dramatic sort. She also had quite the temper. When Charlie messed with her enough, she would cuss him out, throw things at the air where she thought he might be chilling, or even just kick at the air. One time, Charlie threw an empty soda can at Abby, and it hit her in the face. Though it hadn't really hurt, it sure had pissed the girl off.

Charlie had latched onto Abby at this point. He went with her everywhere. He had unhinged her so much now. She would catch glimpses of his silhouette out of the corner of her eye from time to time. He pulled Abby's kayak away from her ex and other friends one kayaking trip and succeeded in making the girl seem completely insane to everyone around her when she tried to explain to them what had happened. By the time this happened, the haunting had been going on a couple of years. Cleo blamed Abby's alcohol intake, which was an easy go-to with Abby's history of bad moments after a few too many. Abby and Cleo were not the couple they had once been now. While they were bound to fail sooner or later, Charlie definitely helped rock that boat. The night things went completely sour for this couple, Charlie was there to help Abby take that mad plunge she took.

CHAPTER 2

The night that Abby and Cleo broke any chance at being one, they were at a party. There were friends, drinking, cocaine, swimming, and some teasing here and there in the pool. Cleo had retired to their bedroom early, and Abby took it as meaning they would sex it up. She had assumed that was why her wife had gone to bed early on. After all, Cleo had been teasing her sexually in the pool randomly, and usually that's what that meant. Things didn't play out that way, though, and when dearly drunken Abby entered their bedroom she got turned down.

One sarcastic response later, and her wife was out of the bed saying that she would be leaving for a few days. Cleo had pulled this "leaving for a few days" stunt one too many times lately, though. The two were fed up with each other, and yet neither one knew how to address it. Abby merely stayed in what had become a one-sided relationship so that she wouldn't have to move back in with her overly religious mother. But now was the breaking point. As Cleo was packing a bag, Abby made a fool's deal with Charlie. She told him that he could have her if he changed her situation. Well, he did, but not in the way that she hoped. Abby got the sudden urge to take the easy way out, see. "I'll show you, bitch," she thundered at Cleo.

Abby ran from the room, and after being with the girl for a decade, Cleo realized what her wife would try to do. She ran after Abby as she bolted to their kitchen. "Ron!" Cleo shouted out to their latest roommate. "Help!" Ron ran after Abby, too, but neither he nor Cleo could get to Abby in time before she'd already grabbed a steak knife and plunged it into her own chest. The two caught up to her just as she did it, and the smile that played across Abby's face haunted Cleo immensely as she called 911 in tears.

Still, the knife didn't kill Abby. She had merely strengthened the bond between herself and Charlie. She didn't know or understand that at the time. She ended up in an ambulance and then the hospital to get all stitched up. From there she was sent to a mental hospital for a week, and then back to live with her dear old mother. Thus, Charlie granted her request and changed her situation. Abby had fucked up, and that was that.

Abby begged God for forgiveness and realized all had been forgiven ages ago. How she understood this she couldn't explain, yet somehow things would be okay. Change needed to happen, and it had. She knew there would be more change to come as well. Cleo had separated from Abby, but that change had needed to happen. The couple even divorced. Yep, in a flash Abby had lost her wife, her sanity, and her pride.

Charlie still haunted her from time to time. He wanted to remind her that he was attached, and try as she did to ignore him, he made that impossible. He even made his presence known to Abby's mother. One day, Charlie pulled back the covers on Abby's bed in her new bedroom when her mom was doing something nice and making the bed for her. Carla had just made the bed, then went to the laundry room for the other blankets, and when she came back into the room, she found the covers all undone on the side that Abby always slept on.

Carla told her daughter about this incident, and Abby realized that something needed to be done about Charlie. She thought it over. Exorcists would only help fellow Catholics, apparently. And they also excluded Catholics if they were lesbian and/or divorced. Abby scoffed and reminded herself that the ones that considered themselves children of the Bible's God had only ever caused her misery and never did help one in need. Yet everyone was a child of the creator, absolutely everyone...entity and human alike.

Abby did a little research here and there, took some walks at her favorite park, and got lost in her own thoughts. As she thought for herself, it came to her. The humans and demons were here together, both cast out of their own paradise, and yet it was said that God is loving and forgiving. Still, he had gifted free will to these beings knowing that they would sometimes do things their own way. Perhaps the whole scenario of them being stuck down here together was a learning experience. Maybe they needed to come together, as equals. Abby needed to come together with Charlie and he with her. They needed to meet in the middle somehow. Abby needed to face her demon immediately. Let's take a look at Charlie's side of things first...

Charlie was rather misunderstood by his own angelic kin. He'd been assigned to one of the weirder humans down on earth, as they called Abigail. "She's an oddball just like you, buddy. You'll fit right in!" Azezal chuckled, to laughs from other newly graduated demons. The lit candles around the dungeon flickered as others laughed at Charlie. He met none of the eyes of his fellow cursed rebels. He knew that they'd never really considered him much of a demon. To Lucifer even, Charlie was a nobody. The one time that Charlie had gotten to meet his hero, Lucifer had shaken his hand without really looking at him.

Charlie's instructor had introduced the two: "This is Rumel, sire. He is one of your rebel angel students, and he has been very eager to meet you." Yet Lucifer had been on his phone, talking business with somebody. He stopped discussing pharmaceuticals long enough to say to the student: "Nice to meet you, Charlie. Keep up the good work," He went back to his phone call, and that was that.

Even the teacher made fun of Rumel for that one. He'd been laughing about it with some other rebel angel teachers while a fellow student had been nearby, and that's all it took. Word spread throughout the school, and everyone called Rumel Charlie from that day on. So, when Rumel got assigned his first human to haunt, terrorize, and maybe even possess, he was just relieved to get away from the others.

As for dearly human Abby...she had been haunted by her demon far too long at this point. She'd ended up living with her mother again, and with that all of her privacy and freedom to really be herself had completely disappeared. Charlie had taken everything from her, and yet he still seemed determined to plague her. Something had to be done.

One night, she called in from her latest job (at a warehouse run by a greedy man who then passed the business on to his even greedier son), told mother dearest to not disturb her, and went into her room. She knew that he'd be there, and as much as she hated the dark, she turned all the lights off and sat on her bed. She only had one form of an incredibly dim bit of light: a candle she'd lit, just so she could see a little bit. She sat on her bed and waited a good couple of hours.

Like most demons, Charlie wanted her to know that she was on his time frame now. Around one a.m., he appeared before her, letting the human see a glimpse of himself. He came out of the air itself it seemed. He seemed to be made of vapor, or colorless smoke. Charlie filled the room with his form and lay down, stretching out comfortably. He loomed over Abby, and though she couldn't see his eyes, she knew that he was looking at her. She knew that the two of them were face to face. She looked at Charlie and simply said to him, "I am not afraid of you."

Charlie stared the human down with a mixture of rage and fascination. Most humans would've either run off screaming or gotten their camera phone and started trying to get the entity on film. The demon was then supposed to disappear as instructed by his or her teachers. Doubt in them brought doubt in God, and that was part of Lucifer's goal. This girl, though, stared Charlie down like he was merely a pet dog who'd misbehaved!

Abby and Charlie stared each other down for what felt like an eternity. Eventually, Abby was the one to break the ice. She spoke quietly, "You know, I get you. You're pissed off. You and your kind...you have free will like we do. Yet, you used it and got cast down. He shouldn't have held that against any of you. I mean, I only know part of the story, but I also know that if God is love, he wouldn't condemn any of us, including you all."

As Charlie listened to the human, his jaw dropped. He masked it as best as he could as she continued to speak, though.

"I just think there's more hope than either of us realize," she finished.

The demon didn't reply immediately. He wasn't quite sure how. This little human gave him a feeling he'd never thought that he'd experience again: hope! He reminded himself of Abby's mother being in the house, though. So when he spoke, he said to the human, "Come to the cemetery where you and your friends summoned me. We will talk there."

Abby watched Charlie's form simply disappear. Should she do this, though? As she contemplated on this, she remembered that she had nothing to lose at this point. So, she got up, grabbed her bag, and left the house. She headed to the dark, spooky cemetery around three in the morning. Her heart pounded like drums at a concert as she parked the car. She got out of the car as her fear of the dark played with her mind. Being alone in this level of darkness, she was screaming inside her own head. While there was a streetlight in the parking lot, there certainly were no lights in the cemetery.

She felt incredibly vulnerable as she slowly entered the old place. She took a few steps into the cemetery; looked around at the trees, tombstones, and bushes that cast shadows here and there from bits of moonlight; and realized that she had left her phone in the car. Still, she chanced a few more steps into the creepy place before abandoning all reason and bolting back out of there to her car. She had reached the car door when she talked herself into going back. "This is my one chance to make peace with Charlie. I need to suck it up and get back in there."

Abby prayed. She prayed for protection from any ill will. She took some deep breaths, turned back, and headed back across the street to the old cemetery. Ignoring her pounding heart, she stepped back inside. She felt like she knew where Charlie would be waiting for her. So she passed countless graves until she got to the oldest part of the place. She made her way to the very spot where she and her friends had used the Ouija board. There sat the form of a tall and firmly built man, though he wasn't solid at all. He seemed like a hologram, really. There was a slight purple tint to his form.

Abby approached Charlie, masking the terror she felt as he looked her way. He seemed to have more of a face this time. He had two dark sockets that were filled with a black emptiness where his eyes should be. The nose and mouth were blackened silhouettes of one bearing the motions of curiosity. Abby stood in place, staring at him with her mouth hanging open.

Charlie spoke: “Have a seat, Abigail.” The human sat on the ground and continued to stare at Charlie with her mouth hanging open. She was speechless. So, the demon spoke again. “I want to hate you, as I was trained to. Yet your words back at your house...they shocked me. They even inspired me. So, little human, this is your chance to explain it.”

Abby swallowed her muteness, and began. “So, we’re in agreement that God gave the humans and angels free will, then?”

Charlie rolled the eyes that Abby couldn’t see and replied, “Yes, yes. So?”

Abby continued, “He then told us all what to do and what not to do—with great consequences if we rebel, right?”

Charlie replied with more irritation now, “Get to the point, human!”

Abby smiled at the demon. She explained, “He wouldn’t have given us free will if he didn’t want us to use it. He cast you all out of your paradise, and us out of our garden, and mashed us all together...as a learning experience. Nobody would subject their children to eternal damnation. No good parent would, anyways, and if most humans love their children too much for something like that...why wouldn't our creator? I could see him punishing some for a period of time, sure. Yet, a God that is supposed to be all-knowing and all-loving would never send his creations that he made flawed to eternal suffering for using the free will that he gave them. I really think he's waiting for some of us to figure that out and figure out how to come together."

Charlie mulled this over, and the more he thought it out, the more it actually did make sense. He asked Abby, "Are you insinuating that the watchers and humans could come together and...what exactly...unite?"

Abby shrugged and replied, "Well, really, why not?"

Charlie shook his head, though, and grumbled something in a foreign tongue, but Abby caught the name Lucifer.

She added, "It is even said in the Bible that God loved Lucifer especially. Why would he favor the one that he knew would betray him? He wanted this. Charlie, he wanted that rebel angel to take the plunge. It's part of his plan."

Charlie shook his head and spoke in English this time. "Lucifer hates Yahweh more than you could possibly know. He will never try for unity."

Abby argued, "As rebellious as he is, why wouldn't he want to shake things up and not go by the Book of Revelation?"

Charlie liked this. He really wanted this idea to come to fruition. Yet the attempt would be beyond scary. He explained as much: "In other words, you are hoping that me and you can go discuss this with Lucifer himself."

Abby nodded to the demon.

Charlie sighed and replied in further explanation, "That is incredibly dangerous—not just for you, but for me too. Can you imagine trying to discuss this with him? Do you know what that could mean for me if he feels that this is an act of betrayal?"

Abby replied, "Betrayal? Do you mean like how he kind of betrayed God?"

Charlie chuckled despite the fears he was feeling. "You have me there, human," he commented.

Abby said, "It's not like your own used their mojo and influence to help add to and take away from the original scriptures anyways...oh yeah, they did. I'm not stupid, Charlie. I know it must scare you to flip things around a little when your kind control so much. I can read between the lines."

Charlie asked, "So you do have some idea of how dangerous this would be, then. My kind...we control everything here, behind closed doors. You would be going against the media, the Vatican, the world leaders, their militaries, and organizations you've never heard of before."

Abby shook her head and explained, "We wouldn't be going up against anyone, though! I merely want an attempt to influence Lucifer for a change in the overall picture."

But Charlie was petrified. He replied, "I just don't know how he will take this."

"The unknown is scary, sure," Abby said. "Still, you try this with me, and don't you think God will consider you redeemed? It's so doable, Charlie!"

The demon muttered back, "The system itself is so much bigger than a little human like you and a novice demon like me."

Abby simply said, "God is bigger than the system, though."

Charlie couldn't deny this at all. He thought it over some more, and finally he cleared his throat and said, "Abigail, I have come to a decision. I will help you get to Lucifer," Abby jumped up and down, clapping a few times. Charlie added, "It is going to be much harder than you think, though. A novice demon like me…I don't even know where Lucifer is right now. We would have to meet up with some friends of mine that are more likely to know his whereabouts."

Abby agreed to this.

Charlie added, "It might not be a bad idea to see if we can influence some other demons first. I think there's a bigger chance that he will listen to you if one of his more respected watchers likes your idea."

Abby agreed to this. She asked Charlie about the friends that might know some locations where the main angel would be.

"I have a dear friend that is human, like you. She is a Wiccan in Louisiana, near New Orleans. She provides the Elite with their human-eating alligators for meetings. Lucifer comes to those meetings; it's just that only one person knows he's there—for now."

Abby did a double take. She repeated Charlie's words: "She's a Wiccan? I'm meeting up with a witch?"

Charlie raised his eyebrows and replied, folding his ethereal arms, “Well, look who’s quick to judge another! Weren’t you just going on and on about how God loves all of us?”

Abby looked at the ground, shuffled her feet, and muttered her reply, “Well, yeah.” She added her other problem to this: “I can’t really afford a trip to New Orleans, though.”

Charlie chuckled and replied, “Oh, silly human! Money is nothing to my kind! I can fund the entire trip!”

Abby looked up at Charlie, eagerly. “Could I quit my job?”

The demon said, “Yes, why not…Abigail, your human worries are so trivial.”

Abby was beyond thrilled. She added as an afterthought, “Just call me Abby, please. I hate the name Abigail.”

Charlie shrugged and said, “Okay, if you say so, Abby.”

The human and demon had agreed to try and bring their kind together now. They’d formed the beginnings of a plan, they’d bonded together, and now the hard parts would start for the both of them. Abby made a joke about requiring a yacht, and Charlie laughed about it and gave her no as an answer. "We like your kind to earn their toys, Abby."

She shrugged and muttered, "Well, it was worth a shot."

Charlie commented, "I do think you should go and get some rest, though. I know your kind tend to need sleep. When you wake up, we will make arrangements to meet with my other human in the New Orleans area."

Abby agreed, then asked her demon, "How will I find you again?"

Charlie explained: "It's simple, really. We are linked. I am a part of you now. I can pop up right in front of you whenever...wherever."

Abby frowned and questioned further, "What do you mean, though: you're a part of me?"

Charlie replied, "Demon anatomy is much different than human anatomy. Seeing as how you gave so little attention to your own kind's science, it would be much too time consuming to try and explain it. Go get you some sleep, and trust that I will come to you once you've gotten your rest."

Abby agreed and watched Charlie in awe as he simply disappeared. The human hadn't realized just how tired she was until she caught herself yawning wide. She got up and headed back to her car. She unlocked it, got inside, started it, and headed home. Once she got in her bed, she was asleep in less than a minute.

Now, allow me to introduce you to the main scoundrels who run this world in secret. They don't go by the Illuminati, as many would think. They are known as the Elite. They threw that business about the Illuminati around Hollywood to throw people off their trail. The Illuminati was simply a name joke to these twisted souls. This was a group of the wealthiest of the wealthy. These were world leaders, heads of great churches, owners of media and pharmaceuticals, and even heads of the mafias. Their leader was Lucifer himself, but the only human that had completely met him so far was one woman in particular. This was who ran the others. Her name was Marie.

Marie owned the satellite manufacturing companies worldwide. She had risen to the top stepping on plenty of balls to get there, and she was not one that anybody wanted to cross. Though many men cowered before this fair-skinned, dark-haired dominatrix of a woman, she was not smiling at the moment. Her office bore the best of everything, including a marble fireplace that had the scene of Pandora's box being opened etched into the mantel. Yet her brown eyes looked hassled and worn out. A black phone with an intercom rang at the desk she sat at. She pressed the button on it and inquired, "Yes?"

A man's timid voice came from it: "Mrs. Marie?"

To this, Marie responded, "Yes, Tom?"

The man announced, "That man is here, the scary one that always refers to himself as Lucifer. He said that he needs to speak with you at once."

Marie sighed in irritation. She knew that Lucifer could simply appear in front of her if he wanted to. She also knew that he loved intimidating her assistant. She replied to Tom, "Send him in immediately! Get his coffee right this time, too, Tom."

Her assistant groaned back, "Yes, Mrs. Marie."

Exasperated, the woman shook her head. She knew that if he was coming right now, she was about to get an earful! See, the Elite had been working overtime trying to bring about the Apocalypse sooner rather than later. Yet, after getting the world's top scientists to create a virus and do this and that to it to make it evolve faster and become more dangerous, it just hadn't killed enough people. The vaccines for this very virus were the next attempt at bringing the people to their knees. Yet there hadn't even been reports of a zombie outbreak anywhere! There certainly hadn't been enough deaths! Lucifer was about to chew her out, and she knew it.

Sure enough, as the doors swung open, his words rang out: "COVID cases slowing down, people still not wearing masks or getting vaccinated...choirs singing again...what the actual fuck, Marie?! You told me that you would have your top scientists on the job, 24/7!" He was seated across from her in no time. How his silvery gray eyes burned through her and seared her with his disappointment mixed with rage.

Marie cleared her throat and replied to the one she adored above everyone, "I am doing everything that I can, sir. We have our Russian lead stirring up trouble with talks of nukes and acts of war. We will bring you your apocalypse, My King!"

Yet the well-kept and silver-haired Italian type looked her over with an expression that clearly meant that it wasn't enough.

Marie added, "We are doing well on our social media end! We've kept the animosities up between the whites and Blacks by giving the Blacks the upper hand now, but only a few of them—to keep the poor ones remembering who to hate! So, we have the people divided nicely!"

Lucifer leaned over slightly and rubbed his hands together. "So, you're doing something right. Is that what you're getting at, my dear? Let me...congratulate you properly." He gave Marie a malicious smile as huge thorny vines sprouted up from the floor on both sides of Marie. These vines rose above Marie, and wrapped around her throat! The vines tightened menacingly, causing her the worst strangling feeling as Lucifer got up from his seat. He left his cup of coffee on her desk. "Keep the coffee. I expect it hotter next time," He paused at the door to her office, and added, "When I come and visit the next time, I expect more deaths. This is my time now, and if you can't keep up, I will find one that can. Planners are a dime a dozen, my dear. I could hire anyone to do it, and they would, for the right price. I encourage you to do better."

Lucifer left, leaving Marie at the vines' mercy. They choked her until she nearly blacked out! Then, they disappeared, leaving the woman clutching her throat and gasping for air. A few minutes later, Marie's assistant poked his head in and asked if everything was okay. Marie responded by throwing Lucifer's cup of coffee at Tom's head in a rage. "It wasn't hot enough! Clean that mess up, and get out of my sight when you are done! I have a lot to do, and I do not wish to be bothered!"

Tom mumbled, "Yes, Mrs. Marie. I'll go and get the towel." He wiped coffee and a little blood from his face where the cup had hit him. He left his boss's office to go get the towel and cleaning supplies. Tom always hated when Mrs. Marie's business partner came for a visit. It was never scheduled, and it seemed to always put his boss in such a venomous state afterward. He came back with the stuff and swept up broken glass in silence as Marie dialed a number at her desk.

As Tom began to dry up the floor, he wondered which language Marie was speaking to whoever she was on the phone with. Her tone sounded awfully anxious for someone who owned the manufacturer of satellites. She gave off major bad vibes as to what she could really be up to. Tom had even let that Russian prime minister into her office on numerous occasions. Why, though? Wasn't he an enemy to their country right now? Tom was too afraid to pry. Mrs. Marie was a sadist, the kind that made other sadists seem timid and sweet. She hired prostitutes from time to time, simply to torture them! According to the media, though, Marie was an absolute saint. She gave millions to the children's hospitals all the time.

What Tom didn't know was that like everyone else, even Marie was sick of the way the world had gotten. The first time she had met Lucifer, he'd made so much sense! A few meet-ups later, he'd brought up his idea to her...one that involved starting the world anew! Marie had been only too willing to help. This Lucifer fellow could do such miraculous things! Marie believed him to be a god—one the main religions shunned for no good reason. She was mistaken, of course. Lucifer had his own plans. The ones that worked for him were nothing more to him than pawns in his chess match against God. The fallen angel, known for his betrayal and known as the main evil, he had gotten a little too wrapped up in himself. He was angry with God for casting him out. Even the reasons for him being cast out had been scrambled around so much, mistranslated, and flat out lied about. God hadn't spoken to him in years. It was maddening! How could he not let his number one know when the end would come?!

Lucifer had gotten fed up! So now here he was, with the best that purgatory could give him. With these Elite stooges, he would bring about the apocalypse on his own. He had misled so many for his own personal gain. Could he be stopped? Better question: Can perfection ever understand imperfection? How easily we do tend to misunderstand each other.

Enough on them for now.

CHAPTER 3

Once Abby had woken up and freshened up, she began packing for her trip with Charlie. She tried to also explain to her overbearing mother that she was going on a trip. It was tricky due to her mother's belief that a lady should never travel alone. Abby couldn't really add, "It's okay, Mom! My demon is coming with me!" Her mother would probably just keel over on that note.

Charlie prompted an idea to her though: "Tell her that you're going with some work buddies," Abby did this, and the conversation went down easier. Once that was handled, Abby checked her bank statements and got a shocker. Her account said that she had a hundred thousand grand in there! As Abby did a double take, Charlie's voice spoke in her head again: "I told you that I can cover you financially. Why did you doubt that?"

Abby shrugged and laughed as the financial stress lifted from her stack of worries for the day. "I'm not use to not stressing about money," she added in her head.

Charlie replied, "I've got you covered, little human." Once things were packed and loaded up in her car, the human told her mother that she was off to collect her work friends for the trip. She hugged her mother and departed from the house that felt more like a prison than a home.

"I sense feelings of a weight being lifted from you each time you pull out of this driveway," Charlie commented from the passenger seat as Abby peeled away. His form was seated and yet hovering right above the seat itself. He looked Abby over as she drove.

The human nodded and replied, "She doesn't mean to hurt me, but all the rules and regulations that she shoves in my face...I can't ever be me, you know? She is constantly smothering me. I like being anywhere but there because—"

Charlie finished her words: "You can spread your wings. You can be yourself everywhere else. I understand. Well, now you get to meet a new type of spiritual people."

Abby grew nervous as she remembered this part, but she drove on. She replied to Charlie with a question, "Could you navigate us there?" The demon agreed.

Abby and Charlie spent hours bonding on this road trip to New Orleans, and the drive went smoother than Abby expected it to, up until Charlie brought up a last-minute point: "Oh, when we get there, I need you to have my friends think that you're Wiccan or Satanist—either or."

Abby began moaning and groaning, and replied, "I don't get told this till now? Damn, man!"

Charlie shook his head and retorted, "Stop belly aching and get with it, human. It isn't like you've never played a part before. I know you have a background in the theater, Abby. Now's your chance to use it! They have the information we need right now, so put your differences aside and just roll with it!" Abby looked pissed. Charlie added, "You want people to respect each other's differences, don't you?"

Abby argued back: "But pretending to be something that I'm not is like a lie. "

To this, Charlie retorted, "A secret agent does it! We are simply getting a location from them, nothing more."

Abby asked the demon, "Why are they raising alligators for Lucifer's forces anyways? You might've told me—I don't remember."

Charlie replied in a rather thoughtless manner, "Oh, it's just for sacrifices or something—don't worry about it."

Abby asked for details, though. "Wait, are the gators getting sacrificed, or are they eating a sacrifice?"

Charlie was starting to find working with a human in this manner to be rather difficult. He snapped at her, "Does it matter right now?"

Abby went quiet for a bit; for she was finding it just as hard to work with a demon. Still, somehow she knew...someone had to try. So, she finally said to Charlie, "Okay, okay. It doesn't matter right now. United we stand, divided we fall."

Charlie felt a smile cross his lips. Somehow, these two would pull this off.

Abby added, "I really don't know much about Wiccans or Satanists, though. So I don't know how to pull off acting like one."

Charlie replied, "Oh, I can walk you through that! We've got an hour or two left before we get there. Let me coach you; it's so easy," Abby thanked the demon and drove onward.

As for Marie...she held a meeting for the Elite, an emergency meeting. It went down the same way: the location was never the same. The only one that knew the location for each meeting was the special driver for each member. All members of the Elite had one of these personal drivers. They'd each been handpicked by Lucifer himself, and unbeknownst to the members, these drivers were not human. The members themselves were supposed to take a sleeping pill of sorts before getting in the vehicle. This tranquilizer was so strong that each human was sure to sleep the whole way to the location. If any member refused to take the pill, they didn't get to go to the meeting.

One ex-member had refused to take the pill once. He had then made the mistake of trying to force his driver to take him to the meeting anyway. He got rough with the silent driver. His driver had crushed his skull in less than two minutes. The public was told that this particular soap opera star had gone missing on a scuba diving adventure in the Bermuda Triangle, but Marie had informed the Elite that he had actually been slaughtered by his driver for refusing to take the sleeping aid and trying to make the driver bring him to the meeting anyway. "I implore you not to do such idiotic things," she told them. "Our king picked each driver himself. Do not make the mistake of thinking you can take one on," That was that.

Now, the meeting itself always started the same. They all would get seated in a dimly lit circular room. The table they sat at would be shaped like a pentagram. In the center of this pentagram-shaped table would be a sobbing child whose hands and feet were tightly bound by rope. Marie would step onto the table and then step down into the center where the child was. She would unsheathe a golden dagger from her petite hip and slice the child's throat. She would collect the blood in a goblet made of cedar. The wicked woman sliced here and there, until there was enough blood inside this cup. Then she would take a sip from it.

She would wave over two servants to come and remove the body of the child and feed it to her gators. She would then pass the goblet around for each member of the Elite to drink of "innocent blood." It was a sacrifice to the devil himself. The children were their animals of slaughter that Marie got from a member who owned the largest child-trafficking business in the world.

After the blood was shed and consumed, Marie would utter, "Praise be to the king who will save us all." The other members would chant, "Praise be!" in unison, and the meeting of the Elite would start. That is how it went this time as well. Marie then looked over at one of their most sadistic and narcissistic pawns in the chess match: the Russian prime minister, Pavlov. She addressed him with "How goes it on your side?"

The blue-eyed menace replied coldly, "I have people running or dying...all of them crying. I have been only sparing the ones that swear loyalty to me. The ones that live on the streets? I collect them, have my butchers chop and grind them up nicely, and then I serve them to my dogs. The Americans and Brits are in a frenzy over all I do to Ukraine. They threaten me with nukes. It is complete chaos, just as you say our king wants. I prepare the way for him always."

Another man with gray hair and beard spoke up: "The media is showing that he is doing this all to gain Ukraine. Viewers attack America's president constantly with comments about how he makes the country look weak. Others are angry with him due to us raising the gas prices and claiming that we'd been getting cheaper gas prices through Russia." The group all laughed with a sickening amusement.

Marie gave everyone a moment to laugh. Once the room had quieted down, she spoke: "While this is all good, it is not enough. We need something that will work faster. Our virus and the vaccines even...they've had such disappointing results."

Her fellow Elite members all quietly murmured to one another. Marie then felt a rather familiar tapping on her shoulder. Lucifer grew impatient. Marie slammed her fist down on the table so hard and suddenly that it made some of the members jump a little. They all quieted down and waited for her to speak. The woman sighed and then spoke with a soft venom. "Our king grows impatient. His enemy, our enemy, they win while we sit idly by on our yachts. We need massacres galore, and soon."

An older North Korean man asked her, "How soon is soon, though?" There were murmured agreements, and a few classy heads nodding.

Marie went quiet as she thought this over. Had there been an exact deadline from her king?

A soothing voice spoke out to the room at large. It was the voice of a man who knew how to play his pawns. It was deep and musical, and it filled the room with its authority: "Two years, my loyal agents…I can give you two years. No more, no less. My enemy is strong. If it takes longer than this, we fail. Free me and my kin from our spiritual hell…we need permanent physical form. You will be given your own kingdoms in the world that we re-create together. Do not dawdle."

Chill bumps ran down the humans' spines as they heard and fawned over words spoken by the greatest deceiver of all time. A well-built Roman who wore nothing but the best called out, "We will succeed! All for you, My King!" There was a wave of clapping from the lot of them.

Lucifer departed, greatly pleased with the adoration that he craved so. Things were about to get very dangerous. There would be even more chaos now—just the way he liked it lately.

As for Abby and Charlie, they had finally reached New Orleans. They checked in at their hotel, and Abby unpacked and grabbed a latte, and then the two headed out again, toward a house in the swamp area that Abby really didn't want to go to. She and Charlie made a little small talk on the way. They had a nice one at first, one where they were agreeing that the animals in the world are treated no better than garbage. Yet somehow the conversation shifted to the plan itself. Abby was asking the demon in a very irritated manner, "Let me get this straight: I am to treat you like a god around your friends here?"

Charlie replied, "Mostly. Don't act like it will be hard for you, Abby. You are an absolute drama queen!"

Abby sighed and murmured, "This is some bullshit."

Charlie shook his head and responded, "Look, just do it so we can get the location of Lucifer. You don't have to get over the top with it or anything. It's not a damn audition for a play, Abby."

The two didn't speak to each other again until they went over a large wooden bridge that led to their destination. Charlie then grumbled, "We're here."

Abby looked out of her car window and forgot her mood as she gazed at slanted trees here and there. The sound of cicadas was as plentiful as waves that crash on a beach's shore. Abby parked farther down once they'd passed over the bridge and got out of the car with Charlie. She followed him down a dirt path that led to a large, two-story house that was black with a gray roof. There was a wooden path that led to wooden steps that went farther down into the swamp. It looked creepier than the house. She was almost relieved that Charlie led her toward the house itself. Near the great gray doors, there was a satanic statue of a well-sculpted man with the horned face of a goat, who held a staff with two serpents wrapped around it. A black pentagram was the knocker for these doors.

Abby took a few deep breaths, and Charlie realized that his human was nervous. He walked alongside her and murmured, "Steady now. Let's just go on up to the door and knock. I'm right here beside you. Guess what? These humans here? They can see me too."

Abby looked over at him and realized that his vapory form had gotten more color to it, and more substance even! He was a grayer, more visible form of a well-built man now! This did comfort the human slightly.

"Okay, okay. I got this," she murmured back with more confidence. Abby and Charlie headed up the steps to the doors. Abby knocked with the pentagram knocker, wearing a look of content. But when a lady with fair skin and short blue-and-silver hair opened the doors, the first thing Abby noticed was the large and ugly tarantula sitting on the woman's left shoulder. Abby's arachnophobia took over all other senses within her, and she backed down from the steps. Instead of a polite greeting, she exclaimed, "Shit! You didn't tell me somebody had a spider here! You two go ahead and catch up or whatever. I'll be back in the car," She began hurrying off.

Charlie spoke with the lady quickly, "Excuse my friend, Kaitlyn. She's new to all of this. I've come to talk a little, but let me go speak with her for a minute and snap her out of her ego."

Kaitlyn gave the demon a welcoming smile and responded, "Ru'Mel! It's always an honor, my friend. I can just go and put Teddy up if your friend is afraid of him."

Charlie loved that she knew his real name. It made him feel...important. He thanked the human and replied, "That's nice of you, Kaitlyn. I'll go grab her and come back in a moment then."

The blue-and-silver-haired Wiccan smiled again and replied, "I look forward to it." She went back inside to put her pet up, and Charlie hurried after Abby in aggravation.

He was in front of Abby when she was but a foot away from the car. "Are you a fool?! Get back over there, and stop acting like a coward! You've made a terrible first impression!"

Abby apologized to her demon but explained, "I'm sorry, man. I just didn't expect a tarantula to be on the shoulder of the girl that greeted us. I'm terrified of those things!"

Charlie shook his ethereal head, and what little Abby could see of his face looked very angry. He replied, "If you don't get over your hostilities—your fears, human—we will not succeed."

How true the words of an angel, fallen or not, could be. Abby knew this. She replied, "Okay, okay. You're right. Let me...let me get ready." She took some breaths to relax herself.

Charlie added, "Kaitlyn also said that she's putting Teddy up."

This should've relieved Abby. But she did a double take. She gave Charlie a look of great distaste and said, "Her spider's name is Teddy?!"

Charlie buried his face in his hands for a moment, dropped the hands back down, and uttered to his human comrade, "Forget the spider, and come on!"

Abby shook herself in disgust, prepared herself for what, in her eyes, was the worst, and walked back to the swamp house with Charlie. As the two reached the doors, Kaitlyn had just come back from putting her beloved pet up. She gave Abby a phony smile and then looked over to Charlie, addressing him: "Ru'Mel! So, what brings you and this...human...here anyways?" She beckoned the two of them inside.

As they entered the place, Abby frowned and started to ask Charlie, "Ru'Mel? You said you're na—" But Charlie replied to her abruptly with a loud "Later. We have so much to talk about, dear human. In the meantime, Kaitlyn, we were in town, and I insisted that my human here meet you. I told young Abby here that nobody could ease her into the Left Handed Path better than you yourself. You have the best herbs and stones around, a great variety of literature, and your mannerisms make you just serene to be around."

Kaitlyn beamed back at the pair of them and led them through a black-walled hallway to a gothic-themed sitting room with black leather chairs around a fireplace that had sigils carved into the brick mantel. The Wiccan told them to all sit down and get comfortable. "Well, I am honored that you thought of me, Ru'Mel. Would your human like some wine or tea or anything?"

Charlie looked over at Abby. She shook her head, though, not trusting this witch at all. "I'm fine, thank you."

Kaitlyn shrugged and replied, "I make the best tea around."

Charlie interrupted: "Actually, I was hoping that you might know where our king himself would be...perhaps where his Elite will next meet. I want him to meet Abby. She has some very interesting things to discuss with him."

Kaitlyn took a seat across from Charlie. She gave him an expressionless look and asked, "That's a big reveal, friend. What kind of things would she have to discuss with him? What interests might this...novice human have that would get his attention?"

Abby could sense a jealousy that boded very ill indeed. She tried to ease into this girl's good graces. "You know, this is the kind of sensitive information that only one as great as Lucifer himself needs to hear. When...Ru'Mel here was drawn to me, he understood that. He told me that he could help, and you are the first one who came to his mind that he said would be helpful, trustworthy, wise, and gracious. Please tell me that you are. This information can bring Lucifer so much."

Charlie loved how well Abby exaggerated the point to Kaitlyn. It seemed to work, even! The

Wiccan was quiet for a moment. Then she smiled at her guests and replied, "Well. You came to the right witch indeed. I have a shipment of my finest alligators going to the Elites' next meeting in a month's time. Why don't you two just ride with me? Our true king will welcome help from any with open arms."

It was agreed to, and a time to be at her home was scheduled

Kaitlyn supplied Abby with some quartz, amethyst, and a little sage, along with one of Crowley's books on magic as a complimentary "welcome to the family" type of gift.

"We will look forward to it, my sweet human," Charlie called out to Kaitlyn, referring to their ride-along a month from now.

The demon and human left Kaitlyn's swamp home with opposite feelings regarding the witch. While she had Charlie fooled, due to using his proper name, Abby didn't trust her at all. She could feel the negative vibes coursing through that woman. Charlie told Abby that she was just feeling that way because the lady had a pet tarantula.

Yet as they drove off arguing about Kaitlyn, the Wiccan herself was proving Abby right. She waited until she'd watched the two pass over the wooden bridge, and then she made a phone call to Marie herself. "I think we have a problem, Mrs. Marie. I think our king has a traitor in his ranks."

Well, Marie was already having a trying time with all of these deadlines with work, along with Lucifer rushing her on the death toll, and now this?! Her alligator provider calling her, Lucifer's head honcho, with this kind if news?! Marie had been drinking mimosas in a nice crystal glass. She dropped the glass as the words Kaitlyn was saying sunk in. "How can you be sure?" she asked the Wiccan girl.

"So, one of his lesser fallen just showed up with this human nobody. She didn't feel right. But he wants the king himself to meet her. He wanted the location to your next meeting."

Marie's eyes narrowed. No doubt, some conspiracy nutjob had caught on to some things and was trying to dig further. Perhaps it was even a couple of nobody reporters. Marie would let them dig, though—their own grave, that is. "What did you tell them?" she asked her gator provider.

Kaitlyn replied, "I told them that they could ride with me to you next month. I thought maybe our king would want to deal with the traitor for himself."

Marie replied with a simple "Fine. Stick to that. Have the authorities follow them around too, in the meantime." These nobodies were nothing to worry about, and Marie would leave it at that for now. She made plans with Kaitlyn on how to deal with a tiny bump in the road, hung up with her, and barked out orders for Tom to come and clean up the broken glass in her office. She would not let anyone she felt beneath her get her down.

As for poor unsuspecting Charlie and his little human, they had stopped at a Cajun café a few miles away from Kaitlyn's to get some of that good and spicy cooking. Things seemed all fine and dandy for them. Charlie was in a random human he'd "bumped into" in the men's room as Abby had entered the cafe. When he'd met back up with Abby at the table she'd been seated at, Abby had made no mention of him suddenly having a physical form. She had no intentions of ruining lunch with that mess. She'd remembered him telling her on their way to New Orleans, though, that demons can't assume a human form for long periods without possessing one. Perhaps it was the only way he could enjoy the foods of the human world. She wouldn't pry right now. Even demons deserved to enjoy New Orleans's best Cajun food. He was rocking some badass black dreadlocks, and not a soul in the place seemed the least bit suspicious as to whether Charlie was actually human.

The two of them enjoyed good food, good conversation, and great beer together. They laughed about laws that made no sense, discussed whether or not coffee required sugar, and went on a long spiel as to how the fashion had changed over time. They were simply like two old friends dining together.

Yet a New Orleans police officer sat a few tables away. He sipped on his latte in silence and acted as if he was looking at a magazine. He never turned a single page of that magazine, though.

When Abby and Charlie were done, they paid for their meal and left the café. The thing is, so did the cop. It was as Abby was heading back to the hotel that they noticed this cop following them. Charlie sat in the passenger seat messing with his human's dreads as he gave Abby directions back to their hotel. Abby brought up the body. "When we park, are you going to let that human you're in go?"

Charlie looked ahead and took a moment to reply. His sunglasses hid his human's eyes nicely at this moment. He finally spoke: "Of course I will—eventually. It could be too obvious to do it when we park, though."

Abby pressed him further. "Come on now, Charlie. You've had your enjoyment drinking and eating the best of New Orleans's drinks and dishes. It's time to let the Jamaican fella go, though." She added, "You act like somebody is even watching us now."

Charlie lit a cigarette and chuckled before replying. "That's because we're being followed. Have you not noticed that the squad car behind us has been on our tail since the café?"

Abby checked her mirrors and went all stony faced when she saw the cop following closely behind them. How could she have not noticed this before? She wanted to slap herself for getting enwrapped in tourist mania instead of playing it safer. Abby sighed and pulled over to the side of the road. Charlie was not happy about this move.

"What are you doing?" He groaned, putting his face in his hands.

Abby replied to the anxious demon, "Don't worry, Charlie. I've got this."

The cop had pulled over behind them. Charlie shook his head in angst as the police officer got out of his squad car and headed over. Abby let her window down.

This cop had a pudge to his stomach, an ugly brown mustache, and a superiority complex. He spoke in a drawl with that southern tang. "Good evenin', folks. Y'all from out of town?"

Abby replied, "Yes officer. We've come from Memphis, Tennessee, to see New Orleans and the swamps."

The cop nodded and then said, "Let me see your license and proof of insurance real quick."

As Abby handed over her ID and insurance card, she said to the cop, "Urn, actually, we are a little lost. Could you tell us where our hotel is by any chance?"

The cop replied, "Let me get your friend's ID too. Once I've checked you two out in the system, if your names clear, I can help you out."

Charlie frowned and replied to the officer, "You didn't even pull us over! We pulled over to figure out where exactly we are."

The cop frowned at Charlie and shot out: "Are you being defiant with me, son? Let me see your ID now."

Abby gave Charlie a pleading look. Charlie wasn't having it, though. He retorted, "No. I'm not even the driver. Are you going to help out a tourist, or are you going to be a bully?" This rebel angel had no clue where this human's ID would be anyways.

The police officer got out his gun and aimed it at the two in the car. He said, "All right, I need you both to step out of the car right now!"

Charlie let out a growl now. It was so inhuman and chilling that it made the hairs stand up on the backs of the humans' necks. He spoke in a much deeper voice now: "Be gone, Officer! Go check on your wife. If you head home right now, you will find her in bed with your brother."

The cop's face went white. He lowered his gun. He handed Abby her ID and insurance card back, said "That will be all," and hurried off to his squad car. He got in and peeled off!

Abby looked over at Charlie in shock. She asked, "How did you do that? How could you have known any of that about him?"

The rebel angel replied, "It's a demon thing. Come on, though; let's get back to the hotel."

Abby started the car back up and headed onward. She commented, "Your kind are so unnerving."

Charlie shrugged, lit another cigarette to enjoy while still in human form, and replied, "You'll get used to it."

Things calmed down after that incident with the cop. Abby and Charlie weren't bothered by the authorities anymore after that, at least for a while. The two enjoyed a couple of days exploring New Orleans's French Quarter, eating beignets, sipping lattes, and admiring the jazzy vibes that filled the place with the best music Abby had heard live in a long time. Since they wouldn't be meeting with Kaitlyn for a month, it came up one night that Abby should find a spot all her own somewhere around there. Charlie told her that he would even pay for it! Abby settled on a place a little more to the south. She got herself a nice cabana on a beach in Key West, Florida. The girl had wanted a spot on the beach her entire life, and now she finally had it. Life was good—well, for a week or so.

CHAPTER 4

One night, after a splendid bonfire on Abby's slice of beach heaven, she and Charlie had retired to their own rooms for the night. As Abby had just gotten nice and comfortable in her waterbed, and Charlie had gotten nice and relaxed in the air of his own bedless demon bedroom, they heard glass shattering in the cabana's sitting room! Abby was on alert immediately. She sat up in bed and got the dagger out from under her pillow. She'd always had a thing for knives and daggers. She was a pretty formidable fighter with them, even. This wasn't going to do her much good with these guys, though.

She heard the sounds of Charlie's door being kicked in first. Some men spoke in a language that she didn't recognize. There was then a sound that seemed like high voltage being used on someone, and then Abby heard Charlie scream. A little bit later, Abby's door was flung off its hinges. Men wearing all black and blackened shades dashed into the bedroom, pointing some sort of guns at Abby! One spoke to her in English, saying to her: "You will come with us, human."

Abby knew immediately that these "men" were demons. She tried to put up a brave front as she stared them down. She asked, "Where is Charlie?"

These demons looked at each other for a minute. One laughed and copied her name for Ru'Mel to the others: "Where is *Charlie?*" The others laughed in amusement.

The legion moved to the side to let another into the room. This big, hulky guy carried a familiar form over his shoulder. It was an unconscious Charlie! How these guys could hold on to his vapory form was just more angel science that

Abby couldn't comprehend, nor did she care to at the moment. "Do not make this difficult. Just come with us," the one carrying Charlie said to her gruffly.

Abby realized that she was in deep now. She sat her knife down on the bedside table and stood up. She asked her captors in a more timid way than usual, "May I change clothes at least?"

The guys laughed. The one who held Charlie replied, "No. That look suits you just fine."

Abby looked down at her attire: white boxer briefs with blue and gold stars jotted all over them, and a white tank top with a blue star in the center that was outlined in gold. She was relieved to see she'd accidentally fallen asleep with her bra still on. She looked at her abductors and said, "Okay. Lead the way," She had no clue where they were taking her and Charlie, but wherever it was must be pretty top secret, because they forced Abby to let them tranquilize her. When she woke up, she was on a pile of hay in a dingy cell. Charlie was not with her. This really worried Abby. At that moment, though, all she could do was sit up, look around a cell with walls of stone, and wonder where the hell she could be.

As for Charlie, he had the first audience with the one who'd had them snatched up. He woke up in his actual form bound to a black iron chair with an otherworldly red substance around him. This substance was used by his angelic kin to keep each other in check if the need arose.

"Charlie, Charlie, Charlie, what are you doing with this human girl? Lucifer isn't very happy with you. My heavens, betraying your own kind? That's not good, buddy." A misty gray spirit sat across from Charlie and spoke these words with curious amusement. The gray spirit bore a pointy horn upon his head, situated where a unicorn's would be.

Charlie knew him. He replied, "Gaap, this is different!"

Yet the other demon shook his ethereal head and made a tut-tut sound.

Charlie tried to explain, "You know how we fear it will end when Yahweh comes back. This girl, though, she believes that there's hope for all of his children, including us!"

Gaap was silent as he processed what Charlie had just said. After a moment, he uttered, "How?"

Charlie replied, "Speak to the human. She explains it better than I would."

Gaap was dumbstruck! How could any of them give a *human* credit for anything? The demon argued back to the schooldays misfit, "These humans are why we are in this situation, Charlie!"

But Charlie shook his head. "Not really, Gaap. I'm telling you, just hear her out."

Gaap was bewildered. This horned being had enjoyed tricking men for centuries! He would bewitch men into loving women that he knew would eventually ruin them financially or psychologically. The ancient Greeks had told fables about a demigod called Cupid. This demigod was about Gaap himself! Yet now a human had the upper hand on Cupid's mind? It couldn't be! "Well. You have my curiosity, Charlie," Gaap finally said to the bound demon. The horned being asked Charlie in his vanity, "So, should I appear as a prince for this lass?"

Charlie replied in agitation, "She is a lesbian, Gaap."

His fellow demon scoffed at his words. He got up and said to Charlie, "Sure she is. Wait until she sees what a beautiful prince I am. She will fawn over me, as all the ladies have."

The cocky demon left the room, had his cronies carry Charlie back to his own dark cell, and prepared for the human girl. His legions were spread out across the globe, due to his rank in Lucifer's forces. Some he kept with him at all times, though. While most were stationed around his columned home, his favorites were his bodyguards and servants. It was some of the personal ones who he had go and retrieve Abby from her cell. In their physical forms, these guards looked like body builders who could break you in half! They didn't say much of anything to Abby. They just went into her cell, and one said, "Come with us." They cuffed her and guided her out of the dungeons, up some stairs, and down a very etiquette brown hallway that had plants scattered throughout the place.

There was a room to the left with lit torches on each side of the door. Abby was led through here, and inside a large pentagram-shaped room. The floor was black marble. There was a black-and-silver chandelier that hung overhead that was very interesting and yet terrifying. It had humans carved around it. They all looked to be in the utmost fits of pain, madness, and heartbreak.

The expressions on each face looked so real. Below this chandelier was a black marble coffee table with a black sectional and two recliner seats around it. Behind the seating area sat an office desk with some books and pieces of paper on it. The chair behind this desk faced a roaring fire in the grandest fireplace Abby had ever seen.

A man's voice addressed the guards from the chair that faced the fire. "Leave us for now." As the guards left, the man remained in this chair, facing the fire. He addressed Abby: "Abigail, come sit down. Let's talk."

Abby prayed a silent prayer to God, asking for courage, and went over to sit on the other side of Gaap's desk. She sat down and waited for whoever was in that chair to turn and reveal himself. The chair whirled around a little later to reveal the most physically fit man that Abby had ever seen. His skin glowed with flawless beauty. It was a bronze kind of tan, nearly. He boasted wavy short blond hair and had the most unusual eyes. They were absolutely mesmerizing, with flecks of blue and gray in them. His muscles were so pronounced that they looked like they'd been sculpted by a very professional sculptor. He wore no shirt and had donned some very pricey black pants. He began the conversation. "So, I am Gaap. I'm the rebel angel that brought Cupid to legend."

Abby sensed that this one liked to brag about himself. Perhaps she could use that to her advantage. She played along and responded, "Wow, I love Greek mythology! What about you inspired them to write up Cupid's stories?"

The narcissistic demon leaned back in his chair and strolled down memory lane with the human. "Since times of old, I have played with men's minds and have caused them to fall for the worst women possible. It's a hobby, really. I appear like this as a human, and…you know, you just can't ever get enough of me."

Gaap waited for the compliment that didn't come. Instead, Abby replied to him, "I don't get it."

Gaap was shocked and hurt at the same time. He stared the pretty redhead down and said, "Well, see, I'm gorgeous!"

"Oh! Okay! For one that's into men, right," Abby replied.

Gaap stood up and showed off his highly toned torso. He asked Abby, "You're telling me that this doesn't excite you?"

"I'm sorry," Abby said. It's just not my thing, sir. It's amazing that you were the inspiration for Cupid, though! Um, did you meet the writers?"

Gaap sat back down in agitation. He replied, "Yes, but never mind that now. Charlie told me that you have some mad idea that includes us fallen ones in a place of happiness at the end of this galaxy's playthrough. I wish to hear this idea for myself."

Abby got serious and began to explain about this hope for happiness for all. "So, humans and angels both have free will, right?"

Gaap replied irritably with, "Yeah, what about it?"

Abby explained further. "God made us both with this free will, okay. But he is also said to be all-knowing."

Gaap sighed and muttered, "This has a point, I take it." He was still fuming that a human female had actually not been attracted to him.

"I promise you, it does, Mr. Gaap," Abby said. "So, Yahweh knew when he gave us all the ability to make our own decisions that we would screw up, a lot. He knew that his favorite angel would betray him and rise up against him. He even knew the things that Adolf Hitler would do! He *knew* how things would play out with everyone. He made all of us anyways. They even call him loving. Tell me why one who is all-knowing and loving, too, would make anyone that would not follow his will. The dying on the cross in the form of a man—I believe that to be for all of us: Christian, Muslim, Jew, even the rebel angel. I believe it simply represents that our punishments…our hells…are in this life itself. No loving creator would condemn those he made flawed to eternal suffering. I can't prove that I'm right, but you know, that's where faith comes in: faith and hope that one truly loving will be better than the average man."

Gaap was quiet for a long time. He sat and gaped at the unusual girl. He put his chin in his hands as he mulled it over. Eventually, he asked, "What about the scriptures that speak of eternal damnation, though?"

"That is not what a loving God would do," Abby explained. "He made us knowing what path each of us would follow. So, he would've known who would accept Jesus, and who wouldn't. Why would he bother to make the ones who wouldn't as different as each culture is in this world? He knew the outcome, so why? I think all of these stories about creation and the flood...they're just stories mixed with truth and lies. They are expected to be followed as guidelines, yet centuries later, we should be thinking for ourselves. The whole thing is a lesson in how to think for ourselves and learn to love one another, despite our differences. If we can unite, we've completed his overall lesson for the here and now."

She added, "He has many names, doesn't he?"

Gaap gazed at the human in awe. How could this be?

Abby went on: "Eternity is eternal, so why wouldn't there be time for all of us to eventually understand the overall lesson? The story about the great flood was told in the story of Gilgamesh even, and that predated the Bible. The Bible's message has been messed with as much as the languages of our world. Your kind spends so much time hating my kind and blaming us. You have us all butting heads about which religion is true, yet if we would just come together and call out to God as a unit...I believe that to be exactly what he's waiting for. He wants someone gutsy enough to try."

The fallen angel got up yet said not a word. He went to the fireplace and stared into the dancing flames. This human made sense, and as much as he hated that, he really wanted it to be true! What would Lucifer say, though? That could be a very big problem. Lucifer had the biggest vendetta against God out of all of them. "My legion guards!" he barked out after gazing into the flames a little longer. Some guards came in immediately. Gaap faced them from the fireplace and said, "Take Abigail here to the more comfortable dungeon."

One of the guards asked, "Do you mean the cleaner one?"

Gaap shook his head and replied, "The one with the bedroom."

The two guards stared at their master in shock. The other asked him, "The nice one?!" to which Gaap barked out, "Yes, you dipshits!" He then looked over at Abby and said in a calmer manner, "I want to think this over a bit more. These two will bring you whatever food and drink you desire while you wait."

The two guards escorted Abby out in shocked silence. They were beyond curious as to who this little human was. But they didn't dare speak to her as they led her to the bedroom dungeon. Once they got Abby inside the bedroom dungeon, she looked around the supposed cell in shock. There was a fireplace, a queen-sized bed with red curtains around it, and an opening in the left corner of the room that one of the guards explained by saying, "Inside there is a human's bathroom." There was even a little end table by the bed that had champagne and a glass resting in a bowl of ice atop it!

The other guard now asked Abby, "So, do you want a steak or something?"

Abby replied, "No thanks. I don't eat meat. If you can bring me anything, though, could I have some vegetable kabobs and a piece of french bread?" The two guards nodded and closed the door. Abby heard several locks click outside the room she was now in. Yet she barely cared as she gazed around a prison cell that was nicer than any bedroom she'd ever had. She went to check out the bathroom, which was also windowless. It was just as nice as the bedroom. There was a clean toilet, sink, fresh bath towels, and even a nice-looking bathtub! Abby hoped that Charlie was also getting this kind of treatment.

As it happened, he was being brought before Gaap now. Gaap had several different rooms and offices in this place. Charlie was brought to the one that seemed to be a space reaching out to the great beyond! The walls in this office were dotted with the stars from the night sky. If you looked at the floor in this office, it made you feel as if you were hovering above the earth itself; it looked like it too. The seating area in this room was in the very center of the office. It consisted of cushions that hovered in the air. These cushions seemed to be made of an orange light. A human would fall right through this kind of seat. They were only for spiritual beings like Gaap and Charlie. With both angels in their regular forms at this time, there was certainly not a problem with this.

Charlie saw that Gaap had his toys out today: a bow and quiver of arrows made of golden light. One sat hovering next to the cushion that Gaap expected Charlie to come to, and the rebel himself already held on to his own set. Charlie floated up to the horned demon and greeted him. Gaap nodded and replied, "Take a seat, and ready your bow with an arrow. We're going to see who can shoot more stars down."

Charlie grabbed the bow and arrows next to the cushion he sat down at. He wouldn't protest. If Gaap was in a mood to play games, that was a very good sign. So, the two fallen angels began their competition. They took turns aiming at the stars along the walls. If one of them hit a star, it would fade away. They did this for a while and spoke of nothing other than the game. Charlie knew better than to bring up any business that concerned a human with Gaap. He would wait and let Gaap himself be the one to bring it up.

The two of them sat on the floating cushions, shooting down stars for a few hours—trying to just feel like some normal fallen angels. They dick-measured about their final shots and laughed as if all were well in the world. Then, Gaap set his bow and arrows down, and they disappeared. Charlie did the same. Gaap began: "Well, Charlie, for once, you've impressed me."

Charlie joked back, "Come on now, I only shot down twelve more stars than you."

Gaap frowned and said, "I mean about the human. Also, you only shot down two more stars than me."

Charlie tried not to seem too excited. He replied, "Was it two? I think you've miscounted."

The horned demon sighed and stared off into space. He commented, "She makes very good points, Charlie. I just don't know how to respond to her idea. I was simply supposed to do away with the two of you. Yet now I find myself wanting to help you get this girl to Lucifer. I feel like he does need to hear her out."

Charlie nodded and asked, "Okay, so how do we do it?"

Gaap replied, "I feel like we should get a few more of us to come together before we try and get Lucifer to listen to her. Let's say we gather at least six more demons to come with us. He'd be more likely to listen if the girl has more supporters."

Charlie didn't like this idea too much. He explained the risk to Gaap: "I don't know about six more rebels coming with us, Gaap. That might look like mutiny to him."

Gaap went quiet. He made a hmm sound as he thought it over again.

"What about like one or two more angels?" Charlie suggested. "That's not going to feel as threatening to Lucifer, surely." Gaap agreed to this.

Charlie asked, "Do you have any in mind?"

"Let's go with one of your school friends, Charlie," Gaap joked.

They chuckled as they remembered how unpopular Charlie had been. This memory gave Charlie an idea, though. He commented to Gaap, "You were the popular one. Why not get one of your old school friends involved?"

Gaap's aura grew brighter briefly as he replied, "Well, that's not a bad idea at all!" These beings' forms tended to dim out or light up from time to time when they got extra excited or depressed.

Charlie asked, "Who was that one you would always get into trouble with?"

Gaap laughed and replied, "Abaddon! We had cleanup duty after class so many times for our pranks!" The memories were very precious to Gaap. He added, "He's the advisor to that Russian dictator now!"

Charlie joked, "Yeah? Who's advising who, then?"

The two of them laughed like old pals. Then Gaap commented, "This is a great idea! We can introduce him to your human—Abigail, was it?"

Charlie replied, "She prefers the name Abby."

Gaap shrugged and replied, "Hmm, okay! Let's go get her and give her the plan, then!"

Charlie eagerly agreed. Things were really looking up now. He ignored that worry in the back of his mind that Abaddon was not going to be good for them to mess with. After all, he'd been inseparable from Gaap back in their school days!

Charlie followed Gaap to go and get Abby. Gaap told his nearest security guards, "We won't need to be accompanied, thank you." The legion didn't question a thing. They simply agreed, as always.

CHAPTER 5

Abby had fallen asleep in the comfortable bed after taking a relaxing bubble bath and dining on veggie kabobs that were possibly the best she'd ever tasted. The young human female was now snoozing away without a care in the world. Due to Charlie and Gaap both still being in their forms of cursed angels, the wake-up call didn't go over very well at first. Abby had only ever seen one demon, Charlie, so while she was used to him...she simply wasn't expecting Gaap to look so much more menacing.

Charlie nudged Abby awake, but as her eyes opened, they caught sight of Gaap's horned form first. She sat up in shock and said, "Jesus Christ!" before she even could get a full analysis of the room and who was in there.

Gaap was rather affronted by her reacting this way upon first seeing his true form, and he glared at her with bared teeth as Charlie tried to brush things off. Charlie explained to the startled human, "Whoa whoa whoa! This is Gaap, Abby, in his true form. All is well, I assure you!"

Abby and Gaap took each other in, and Gaap tried to start anew with the human, commenting, "I merely look like this due to the Jesus you speak of cursing our appearances after the Fall. Anyways, Charlie here tells me that you prefer vegetarian foods, so I have biscuits and coffee for you in the dining hall. I have decided to help you with your idea and would like to discuss plans for bringing in another angel or two before we bring you to Lucifer himself."

But Abby's eyes were glued to Gaap's horn. Well, Gaap noticed. He finished addressing her with, "Will you stop staring at my horn, ma'am?!"

Abby shook herself to snap out of it and said, "I've just never seen something with a horn that isn't, you know...rocking two horns."

Gaap replied indignantly, "It is a very nice horn, thank you, foolish mortal girl. Why am I even agreeing to help you?"

Charlie intervened. "Let's not get ahead of ourselves, okay?"

But Gaap shot out at Abby, "Oh, and your hair looks terrible when you first wake up."

Abby fired back, "Okay, you horny ass clown."

Charlie shouted over the both of them, "Enough! Both of you! Down here, time is precious!"

The other two glared at each other, but didn't continue acting rude with each other. Gaap calmed himself as much as possible and then spoke to Abby again. "Anyways, I liked what you explained last night. Get yourself freshened up and then knock on your door when you're ready. One of my legion will be out there waiting to escort you to the dining hall, where we can discuss things in more detail."

Gaap left first, but Charlie hung back long enough to speak privately with Abby. "Do try and not piss off the only other demon you have on your side right now. This whole thing could go wrong in a snap of a human finger, Abby."

The human agreed and replied, "Okay, okay! I was just kind of shocked with that horn. It's my bad, Charlie."

Her number one comrade warned her, though: "You can't be acting jumpy or disgusted every time you see a new demon. In these cursed forms, we all have some flaw or other. It's part of our punishment. You will see some of us with hooves, some of us with snouts, and even a few of us with beaks."

Abby replied, "I will act like it's not such a shock next time."

"See that you do," Charlie said. "We are very prideful about our appearance. We were the most beautiful before we rebelled." Abby understood about being prideful about one's appearance, and she said as much.

Charlie nodded and headed to the door. "Okay. Get cleaned up and choose some clothes from that wardrobe over there."

He left the room, and Abby turned her attention to a wardrobe in the far corner of the room.

It hadn't been there before. She went over to it, making a mental note to be nicer to Gaap in the future. Their allies were rather slim. She settled on a very cute green baby doll dress with matching heels. She put it on after taking a quick shower and dealing with her hair and teeth. Someone had great taste in fashion, Abby decided, as she donned the dress and shoes. She checked herself out in the floor-length mirror in the bathroom and smiled as she noticed how well the green went with her auburn curls. She was officially ready for coffee and plans now.

Abby knocked on the door to what had been her prison and was greeted by one of Gaap's legion rebel angels. This one had the typical physical form of a hard-core bodybuilder, but there was a sincere manner about him. He looked Abby over and commented, "This is the first time I've ever seen your like knock on your prison door with me under the authority to let you out and lead you with no chains to my master. From prisoner to guest—you are indeed rather unusual."

Abby replied with reddened cheeks, "I'm not that bad, once you get to know me."

The guard cracked half a smile and then asked, "So, are you ready for me to escort you to the dining hall?"

Abby gave him a nod and replied, "Lead the way."

This legion guard was the first to actually speak with Abby like she was more than just a prisoner. This felt like a step in the right direction. She tried to keep it up as the two of them walked down the hallway. "So, what do you do for fun?" she asked him casually.

The guard gave her a funny look and replied, "That is not your concern, human."

Abby shrugged. "Oh, okay." She tried to keep it going, though. "I like to bodyboard."

The guard tut-tutted. "I can be the wave itself, if I want to, silly little mortal."

Abby commented, "Wow, that's awesome!"

This flattered the guard immensely. He grinned as they turned into a hall that had no rooms other than a pair of black doors with golden knobs at the end of it. Torches hung from each side of the walls and let off a dim light that made the hallway's vibe majestic in a very ancient manner. "The dining hall is beyond those doors. Gaap and Charlie are already in there waiting on you. Is there anything else you require?"

Abby gave the guard a smile and replied, "No, no thank you." She walked down a ways, toward the doors, and then looked back at the guard and commented, "You should take yourself a break. Go be a wave for a while, and enjoy yourself."

The demon stared at her with a mixture of emotions: shock, curiosity, and happiness. Abby went into the dining hall, and as the doors closed, the demon felt an uncommon fondness for her. "Not too bad, for a human," he muttered to himself and went to take a break after all. Just the idea of a break from constant, monotonous guarding was such a unique thing for him, something he was unaccustomed to. It brought him a little bit of joy. Indeed, how nice it was to just sit his human down in the courtyard, light up a cigar, and do nothing else other than puff on it.

As for Abby and her new partners, they had plans to discuss, and the human needed caffeine to consume. The dining hall was as grandiose as the rest of Gaap's fortress home. It held a great table for feasting in the center of the hall. The table was rectangular and fit for a king! Behind it was an enormous fireplace, in which a roaring fire danced merrily. Abby chuckled as she came over to where the two demons sat in their chairs that hovered above the ground. She sat across from them in a regular chair and began to pour herself some coffee. She was able to fix it exactly how she preferred it: cream, sugar, and expresso. She was still giggling slightly as she drank it, though. "What is it with you and fireplaces? You have one in every room I've seen so far."

Gaap stared at her in silence. Charlie gave Abby a very agitated look, and she quickly added, "I am sorry about earlier, Gaap. Your horn is actually very artistic. It's sharp!" She hoped that this compliment would suffice. She even brought in some more compliments. "It makes me think of the great columns that hold up all of our world's best-looking buildings. Great coffee too."

Charlie nodded his approval to Abby as Gaap replied, "Well, my horn is the only one like it. Our other kin that bear horns always have two on their heads. Some curve up; some curve downward. I just have the one, though, slightly spiraled. It's on the center and has a very sharp tip."

Charlie cut in now, fearing that the human would start laughing due to the way Gaap's boasting was worded. "So, are you ready to hear about the other fallen angel we would like you to talk to?"

Abby sipped on her coffee and listened attentively as Charlie explained how he and Gaap felt that the more demons were with them, the better their chances. Gaap threw in a tidbit: "We settled on at least two or three more, but no more than that. We certainly don't want Lucifer thinking it's a mutiny."

Charlie added, "We have settled on Gaap's old school friend."

Gaap nodded with great gusto, adding, "He goes by Abaddon. He is an angel of destruction, and one of my best buddies from back in the day."

Abby nodded, poured more coffee, and asked Gaap, "Great! So, where are we meeting him?"

Gaap replied, "Moscow, Russia! He is the advisor for that country's leader."

Abby couldn't hide her shock at this reply. She stared at Gaap and Charlie with a look of utter horror upon her face. "Russia?! The Russia that my country is fighting right now? You can't be serious! He is that asshole's advisor? I mean, I'm not even dressed for that climate. It's as cold there as its people are!" She moaned and groaned and continued blabbering: "Please think of someone else! I know that there have got to be demons all over the world!"

Charlie retorted to the panic-stricken human, "I've told you that this wouldn't be easy! You need to pull yourself together. Turn the other cheek at whatever you have against these people, and focus on the mission!"

Gaap added, "He is one of my best friends. I have complete trust in him, Abby. It won't even take but a few seconds to get there by human time. I am quite gifted. I got top marks in my classes on forming monoliths!"

Abby asked, "What's that?"

Gaap explained, "You can teleport through them." He boasted, "Lucifer himself gifted me with those."

Abby scooted away the plate of biscuits that she had been considering. She suddenly wasn't too hungry. Her nerves were all over the place now. She told her comrades, "Fine, fine. When do we leave?"

The two fallen looked at each other as they thought this over.

Abby felt like she'd just asked when she was going to die. "Lord, give me strength," she prayed in her head. She felt a sudden feeling of warmth and comfort wash over her.

Gaap finally said, "I am going to pay him a visit after this, and I can see when he has time for a private meeting with us that way."

This was agreed to by Abby and Charlie, and that was that. Abby finished a third cup of coffee, and then asked Gaap, "Do you have a path somewhere for a little walk that I can take?" Charlie gazed at her with a hurt expression as she added, "Privately?"

"Why, indeed I do!" Gaap replied. "I have the most marvelous garden with a little brick path that goes around a pond. It's toward the back of my fort. Have one of my guards take you there, and they will leave you to your private walk if you feel confident that you won't get lost. The pond is rather large, see."

Charlie asked Abby, "Are you sure that you want to go walking along an unfamiliar area alone?" It was an almost brotherly concern that he had in his tone.

Though Abby could sense that, she gave him a smile and replied, "I just want to be alone with my thoughts for a bit."

Charlie looked at this human that he felt he'd taken in as a sister. He nodded and said, "Well, okay then, Abby. I'll just wait here. Call my name if you get into trouble or get frightened at all."

Gaap chuckled and chimed in, "Charlie, Charlie! She is in my home and is no longer my prisoner, but my guest! Therefore, she is perfectly safe! I am not going to be long at all, you two. I'm simply popping in on my old buddy long enough to schedule a meeting for us all. I am going to let you both know when the meeting will be, the moment that I return. You two just relax in the meantime. Make yourselves at home!" Gaap then floated up above his hovering seat. He formed one of the monoliths he'd spoken about. It looked like an actual hole in the atmosphere itself, and it made a faint sucking sound. Gaap stepped into it, and Abby and Charlie silently watched it close up around their newest partner. Not even a second later, it didn't even seem like there had been a funny-looking hole there, or a demon stepping through it.

Abby and Charlie looked at each other now. Somehow, the two of them had become rather great friends. Charlie could sense the human's stress and fear for the future. He said to her in complete honesty, "You really are a strong woman for your size. Even when I was haunting you, it impressed me how tough you were."

This little bit of encouragement made Abby smile. She nodded, got up from the table, and replied, "I'll only be a little while. Thank you, Charlie," Once she got to the doors to the hall, she added, "It's a good thing that it was you that haunted me, and not another. Had it been a different one, this thing we're trying to pull off might never have happened."

Charlie had a rather remarkable face, one mostly hidden by God nowadays as a punishment. Right at this moment, though, it held a smile. Now, Charlie could form a fake face and body whenever. Yet none matched the true face that had been taken from him. It had held such depth! His eyes had been dark and yet light at the same time. If you could see them now, you would see an entire galaxy resting within them. That's another story though, one for another time, perhaps. He called after Abby as she left, shouting out, "Be careful out there then."

But Abby knew to be careful. She chose the guard that she'd had a conversation with earlier to lead her to the garden, for at least she'd kind of warmed up to him, she felt. This guard was happy to help. He told her that he would lead her there and back if she preferred. She thanked him graciously.

The guard took her to the loveliest garden she'd ever been to. The pond itself was the size of a lake. There were marble columns covered in ivy that wrapped around the courtyard that separated it from being completely outside the fort. There were statues of obsidian and sapphire among the flowers. These statues displayed satyrs chasing nymphs, Cupid aiming his bow at a mortal man eating an apple, and even Hades himself snatching up Persephone! The statues all were placed in such detailed story settings that Abby found herself smiling despite her fears of going to Russia. Pavel Stepanov, that wicked dictator, wasn't scary in this place.

Abby walked past lovely willow trees and lotus flowers of pastel colors. She left her fears behind her. She gazed at lily pads in the pond and saw a frog here and there. Those frogs didn't have a care in the world. There were the most stunning sparkles among strange purple and white blossoms that grew along half of a big old log that was sticking partially out of the pond. "Even the most wretched bud can blossom into something magnificent." As Abby said this aloud to herself, she reminded herself, too, of something: the chance of running into Russia's wicked dictator, Pavel, was pretty unlikely. Gaap was speaking with Abaddon right this moment about when the best time would be for them all to get together and speak privately. With the two of them being old school buddies, there was a certain amount of trust there. Things would be just fine other than the cold that Abby figured would come from simply being in Russia.

She finished her walk in a much better mood and found the guard she'd befriended waiting for her at the entrance to the garden path. "Are you ready to go back?" he asked.

She gave him a warm smile and replied. "Yes. Thank you." She asked the guard, "So, what name do you go by?" She hoped that he'd share a little of his story this time as he led her back toward the dining hall.

"I go by Rahj," he said. "Being one of Gaap's legion kin feels like it's been my whole existence. The events before our fall happened so long ago. It's hard to remember what I even looked like before the great war."

Abby could feel a pain in his words. She replied in a soothing manner, "You know, I think we're all just in a period of purgatory right now. The humans, the fallen angels...I feel like it's simply God's way of teaching his most boisterous rebels. He made us all imperfect. He's teaching us through us learning from each other. He simply watches in silence as we continue."

Rahj scoffed. "God is no friend to my kind," he said.

Abby answered him with confidence. "I disagree, Rahj. If God truly loves like a creator should, he will forgive all of us, even the fallen. He knew that you would do what you did, so why make you in the first place, knowing that you suffer forever due to you going your own way? He gave us the ability to do so. I think he is simply teaching us cause and effect."

Rahj didn't argue with this by any means. He thought over her explanation in silence as he led her the rest of the way to the dining hall. Upon getting her back to the door, he said to the human, "Just between me and you, I hope you're right." Rahj then walked away from the unusual human without another word. Abby went back into the dining hall to find that Gaap had returned and that he and Charlie were sitting in their special seats discussing random demon things as they waited for her.

Abby kept herself free from how out of her control this quest was getting. She walked over to where the two demons sat waiting for her and asked Gaap, "Okay, I'm back. I see you are too. You've got a pretty nice garden to walk around. When are we meeting your old school friend?"

Gaap beamed at Abby due to her compliment. He replied, "My statues out there were custom made for the garden itself, you know. It's nice that you have good taste in art. So few mortals do anymore. Oh, and we will all be joining Abaddon for dinner this evening! He is going to have a host for me to possess, and one for Charlie as well, so that we too can taste the foods that we so often don't get to taste. It will be quite a treat. He told me that he will have the finest wines imported from Italy, the best cheeses, chocolates, and a great boar too!"

Abby shuddered at the thought of Pumba staring at her from the table.

Charlie muttered to Gaap, "Abby is a vegetarian."

Gaap nodded. "Oh, you might've mentioned that before. Never you mind, dear! There will be breads and potatoes, and maybe some green vegetables even!"

Abby smiled at Gaap and gave a half-hearted "Yaay" for a response.

Charlie brought up something else to the human. "Why don't you go see what we've placed in your wardrobe for Russia's climate? You've got plenty of time now."

Abby was pretty curious about what that could consist of.

Charlie added, "Oh, and when you're ready, Gaap here has some weapons for you to look over, just in case things go sour."

Abby's eyes lit up at the idea of a fallen angel giving her weapons to choose from. She replied, "Could I see the weapons first?"

The two demons lowered their seats back to the ground, and Gaap took the lead. He said, "I have a very special room for weapons. Actually, I have two rooms devoted to weaponry, but one is for angels only. Come with me to a mortal's playground, though." He led his skeptical demon and a very excited human out of the room they'd been in, down a few halls, and then through a random wall that became a staircase as they stepped through the wall.

Charlie put on a high-pitched voice as they followed Gaap up the staircase. "Oh, gee, what a treat! Cupid is taking me to his own personal armory! I could just die!" Gaap made to push him back down the stairs, but they were just messing with each other.

These stairs looked like the starry night sky, and they went up a few flights. At the top, the floor and walls were golden, making it seem they had climbed steps in space until they had reached heaven. There were two different doors to choose from in this particular hall. Gaap led them past the first door and down to the second one. This door was black and had a triangular-shaped doorknob. Gaap gave Abby a prideful smile, opened the door for her and Charlie, and said, "Après vous."

As they entered the room, Abby barely noticed Gaap mention that he needed to go into the angelic armory next door real quick. She was too busy drooling over the shelves that held knives, daggers, rope, chains, and even dart guns. There were replicas of knights that held axes and ball and chains. There were swords in glass cases, and all along the walls were bows and quivers of arrows. The bows were all different shapes and sizes.

There were rows of cannons, whips, cases of shotguns, revolvers, and even bazookas! As Abby was looking over the interesting designs on some shields, Gaap returned with a funny-looking emerald-green vial that had a picture on it of a cat with three eyes. Charlie was chuckling at the look of wonder on Abby's face as she gazed over at a section that was reserved for grenades and other explosives. "I think she really likes this room, Cupid," he told Gaap with a laugh.

The demon smiled and headed over to the human. He handed Abby the vial he was holding and said, "You will only use this on beings like myself, and only if you absolutely have to. You simply get it out of your pocket and throw it at the one that is trying to hurt you. What is inside the vial will do the rest. Oh, and stick to weapons that are easy to conceal. I imagine we will certainly be searched."

Abby looked over the green vial and asked, "What will it do?"

"Don't worry about that part," Gaap said. "Let's focus on which weapon you want to stow away for humans."

Abby replied, "I'm pretty partial to some knuckles, if you have any."

Gaap chuckled, repeating, "If I have any! Madam, you wound me. Come this way!" Abby followed the demon to yet another glass case. This one held pocketknives in every color along with a variety of knuckles. He got out some black, diamond-encrusted knuckles that seemed to have a knife built in to them as well. He gave them to Abby and said, "All you have to do to use the knife within them is swish downward. Be careful, though. That knife could cut through steel! I'm not even kidding."

Abby approved of this two-for-one weapon completely. Still, as Gaap handed her an extra vial of that funny powder in the green vial, she asked, "Why are you preparing me for a fight if you trust this demon?"

Gaap shrugged. He casually replied, "It *is* Russia."

Abby hated how much sense that made nowadays.

Gaap and Charlie looked Abby over as Charlie spoke up. "If you're ready to find an outfit now, I do think this is the safest amount of weapons that you should be bringing."

Gaap agreed and added, "You will want to find an outfit that hides the vials and knuckles completely. We don't need to see any bulges at all."

Abby agreed, wondering if this was what it felt like to be a secret agent at all. She asked her two spirit comrades, "So, does your friend speak any English?"

The two demons laughed their asses off. Abby's face went red as she waited for them to stop with the laughing. Charlie finally said, "He's an angel, Abby. Fallen or not, we know languages that would make your kind speechless."

Gaap added, "He speaks better English than most of you Americans!" He was still laughing.

Abby got a little huffy now. She said, "Your culture is pretty new to me, guys. I mean, it seems like you know more about my kind than I do about your kind!"

Gaap boasted back, "Of course we know more about humans! We shaped you. For centuries now, we have whispered ideas and plans into investors' and leaders' heads! We formed your society!"

Abby found this unnerving. She turned from the demons and said, "I'm gonna go find my outfit."

Gaap seemed to like going into overkill. He called after her retreating back, "Our kind whispered the ideas into the heads of your fashion designers too. We have been deciding what's a trend every single year!"

Charlie argued with him. "Actually, a few of the styles that our kind have approved of were originally human ideas."

Still, Gaap scoffed. He insisted, "Far and few, Charlie! I could count them on human hands."

The two entities launched into a debate about this very thing as Abby escorted herself back to her room. Somehow, she was finding her way around Cupid's fort much better now. When she opened up the wardrobe in her room, she noticed that the selection had indeed changed. There were snow pants or cargo pants to choose from. They were all a variety of colors and seemed to not just hold pockets. They held pockets within pockets. There were so many hidden pockets that not even a member of the Secret Service could possibly find them all! The shirts were all crew necks or cardigans, and they came in every color as well. They had a certain shimmer to them, and it gave their looks some class. Abby imagined that was expected of anyone going to dinner with angels. There was a variety of hats, gloves, scarves, and boots to choose from too.

In the end, the mortal girl chose black pants with a black cardigan that had white trim. She donned a black muffler hat and matching black boots that just happened to be steel toed. She knew that steel-toed boots would have more umph if she needed to kick somebody with them. After a hot shower, she fixed her hair, put on the outfit, and put the two emergency vials in her pockets within some pockets. She put her knuckles in a different hidden pocket and then checked out her reflection. She was relieved to see that there were absolutely no visible bulges whatsoever.

Abby met up with her demons in one of the sitting rooms that Rahj told her she could find them in once it was closer to time for the dinner date. The two were sitting by a roaring fire in a stone fireplace. "Cupid and his fireplaces," Abby thought to herself in slight amusement. As she approached him and Charlie, Gaap commented to her, "Looks nice. Are your weapons hidden already?"

Abby grinned and asked, "You mean you can't tell?" She whirled around dramatically and added, "I do indeed, sir demon."

The two angels nodded their approval, and Charlie asked Abby: "Are you ready to dine with angels, little human?"

Abby swallowed her nerves, and then answered, "Let's do this."

Gaap gave some instructions now on the use of monoliths. "So, once I make this monolith, Abby, you will need to hold our hands as we go through it. Do not let go until we have reached the other side."

Abby frowned. "But how do I hold the hand of beings that have no physical form?"

Charlie explained, "Remember when I was haunting you? Do you recall the time that I scratched the mark of the beast onto your hip while you slept? My kind can form physical connections with those we haunt."

Abby nodded but asked, "What about Gaap?"

Gaap replied, "Ohh, I see what you mean. So, you will hold Charlie's hand, and he will be holding my hand. That's fine. The important thing is just not to let go until we've reached our destination." He sounded so serious about this.

Abby agreed and was too nervous to even ask what exactly would happen if she were to let go. She didn't intend to let go of Charlie's hand until these angels told her that it was okay to do so. She asked them, "Can we just get this part over with?"

Charlie gave her a warm smile as Gaap replied, "Great!"

The demon stepped away from the other two and began making motions with his arms like a music conductor would. Abby's jaw dropped as the atmosphere by Gaap seemed to literally rip itself open! She gazed at the gaping hole of black nothingness. "How did you do that?" she exclaimed.

But Gaap shook his head. "No time. Let's link hands—come on!"

Charlie grabbed hold of Abby's hand, and Gaap grabbed his. Then, they stepped through the monolith in sync. Abby saw a fleeting glimpse of oceans, planets, and stars. She gripped Charlie's hand tightly as she got the feeling of utter weightlessness. Then it was over!

CHAPTER 6

The three of them stepped out of the monolith onto a cold and snowy street in what was clearly a very wealthy neighborhood. There were trees that had lost their leaves blocking the other homes from view, but the great black gate that stood in front of them told Abby everything. Behind this gate was a manor that made other mansions seem like shacks in comparison. Gaap saw the look of awe on Abby's face and muttered, "Yeah, Abaddon likes to show off."

They let go of each other's hands and walked up to the closed gate. An overly muscular sort of man wearing a black trench coat and a black furry hat looked down at them from the other side of the gate. His skin was the color of sour milk, as was his attitude. His cold gray eyes looked them over, and he said something in Russian. Gaap replied to him, but in a completely different language. Whatever he'd said in whatever language that was caused the guard's expression to change. He backed away, waved to someone to open the gate, and once the gate opened, he beckoned them all in.

As they came through the opened gate, this guard spoke to them in sudden English. "I had been told that Mr. Abaddon would be expecting some company over for dinner. Follow me into his home, but I ask that you touch nothing."

The three of them murmured their agreement before the guard led them down a snowy path and then up the stone steps of Abaddon's grand manor. Abby gazed at a home that was grander than any she'd ever seen before. Inside, it was spacious and filled with statues. In the main hall alone there were six chandeliers! The guard led them down a columned hallway, up a grand staircase, and through a darker hall. Random human heads rested in glass cases here. One had leeches all over it, and yet another seemed to be a shrunken head! The guard looked back at Abby, saw what she was staring at, and commented, "My employer really likes his art. Your kind, the faces are all so classic, so animated, so unique."

They heard a man screaming out in agony behind the wall they passed. "What's that about then?" Abby asked the guard.

He looked her over and almost didn't reply. Yet he apparently loved the human reaction. So he said, "Mr. Abaddon experiments with new ways to torture the human body. He shows off his favorite methods to his buddy, Pavlov. Every now and then, he lets his legion guards take a swing at it for fun. What is with the look of disapproval? The one that's in there right now is a bum we found taking a shit by a dumpster this morning. He is in the way of society. My fellow legionnaires are in there entertaining themselves with the man. Maybe we could let you take a whack at him."

The guard laughed and looked at Gaap and Charlie, clearly expecting them to laugh as well. "Picture it! A little American woman hacking at a bleeding lump of a man!"

The other two demons laughed along with this demented guard to save face. Abby could sense their uneasiness, though. She did hope that this legion dog was too daft to notice this. He led them around the corner to a door of solid gold. It had funny writing on it, but the doorknob itself was a pentagram. Before he opened this door for the three of them, he explained to Gaap and Charlie, "Your human hosts will already be seated at the table inside. Enjoy dinner!"

Even though Gaap could don his own human appearance with ease, like the other cursed fallen, he could only enjoy smelling and tasting by possessing a human. His appearance as Cupid was only ever just a façade. So, as the doors opened, Gaap was in the room before Abby had even taken a step. A man's booming laugh echoed throughout the dining chamber as one of the two drugged men suddenly seemed to come to life. The "man" began piling the golden plate in front of him with everything from wild boar, to deviled eggs, roasted duck, and potatoes! He poured wine into his goblet as he shoveled cheese into his mouth. He then murmured a greeting to his old school friend. "Hello, Abaddon. Been truly looking forward to this!" Gaap was in utter paradise as he used his human host to tuck in.

Charlie tut-tutted from the other human host at this point. He commented to Gaap, "You give nobody time to get seated and choose their human host in a more civilized way."

Abaddon stopped laughing and Gaap stopped eating long enough for the two of them to look over at Charlie, who was inside a frail old man with wrinkles and a white beard. Then the two looked at each other wearing younger, healthier men with yellow hair and all their teeth intact. Gaap and Abaddon erupted into fits of laughter that brought them back to their good old days of demon school. They'd always been a pair of cutthroat cutups.

Charlie shook his human's head in mild irritation and began loading up his own plate with food. Every time he moved this old man's arms, he could feel the aches and pains of a human's arthritis.

Abaddon finished laughing, and spoke to them. "It does me good to see the two of you again." This particular demon had been in Russia for so long, he'd adopted the accent as his own.

Abaddon then noticed that the human Gaap had been so eager for him to meet was still standing at the entrance to his great dining chamber. He hated her immediately. "Human!" he roared, causing Abby to jump.

She looked over at the latest cursed angel. He was beyond frightening. Though he wore a godfather-looking flesh bag, his negativity shined through those cold eyes, and there was absolutely no love for anybody in there.

Abaddon spoke to her in a fake calm manner now. "Come on over here and socialize. Have food! Have drink, dear! There is plenty for all of us! I won't bite you even…yet." He chuckled at his own joke.

Abby smiled at the demon, masking her fear very well, as she headed over to the large table. She tried to sit next to Charlie, but Abaddon called out to her: "No, no, no, no. You will be sitting by me. Gaap has told me that you have things you can enlighten me with! I want to hear all about it. It's not every day that a *human* fascinates my buddy Cupid over here."

Abby gave him a polite nod and went to sit next to this new and frightening demon. She watched him rip into the meat of a turkey leg as she got situated.

"Tell me what you're called," Abaddon said to her, in between bites.

"I go by Abby. You?"

The demon poured a full glass of red wine and offered her the drink in a rather forceful manner as he replied, "I am Abaddon. I have served Lucifer himself longer than you have been alive. Drink this!" His pride was so great that he might as well have been wearing a shirt that read *I'm the greatest!*

Abby put potatoes, broccoli, mushrooms, and peas on her plate as she said, "Ohh! Wow" to fake being impressed by this cocky angel's statement.

As she grabbed a roll, Abaddon studied her with a great frown upon his human's face. He questioned her eating habits, commenting, "Aren't you going to have some of the boar or duck? I have turkey legs, lamb, deer." The other two demons had busied themselves with their own plates and paid Abby and Abaddon no mind as they enjoyed a pleasure lost to their kind after the great fall.

Abby replied to Abaddon, "I don't eat meat."

Abaddon stared at her in silence. She realized that he was going to be a tough one. She explained, "I mean, I don't look down on those that do eat it. It's just not my thing."

Abaddon watched Abby intently as he chowed down on roasted duck. He replied, "You don't like that the animal in question felt the stroke of death take them, yeah? I imagine that it turns your stomach when you think about how many cows are slaughtered in your country each year for the mere satisfaction of the typical fat American. Had you watched a video on how they do it, then?"

Abby took a swig from her wineglass as she wondered if this demon was toying with her.

Abaddon stood up and asked her, "Would you like a demonstration? Perhaps a little *entertainment* before you dine."

Abby pushed her plate of food away as Abaddon went to a space in front of the table and clapped his hands twice. A monolith appeared, and a butcher stepped out of it with a cow. Abaddon sat back down, chuckling. "Go ahead and kill this beast for our audience here," he instructed the hooded butcher.

Charlie stopped eating, finally realizing what was happening. "Abaddon, knock it off. Come on—bring in some dancing women or something. Abby is fond of the ladies like we are!" This is what he said to Abaddon, and his words had the butcher lowering the axe he'd raised above the doomed cow.

Abaddon looked over at Charlie in shock. "She likes women? Wait, is she a lesbian?"

Gaap stopped eating now, trying to find a way to save the situation.

Abby glared at Abaddon. He had fueled her rage, which was his specialty. She shot out, "Yes, I am lesbian, and vegetarian! So what? You betrayed God himself, yet *I'm* not judging!"

Abaddon's host's face grew very red. He angrily got back up. He went over to the butcher, grabbed the axe from him, and chopped him to bits.

Gaap cried out to his friend, "Abaddon, what are you doing?! Stop it, buddy! You haven't even heard her out!"

But Abaddon paid his old friend no attention as he then proceeded to behead the cow. Abby felt the tears stream down her face. Abaddon said to the three of them, "She cries more for the cow than she does the man! So, you think you are better than me, Abby?!"

Charlie and Gaap both got up and went to stand next to the sobbing mortal. "Enough of this shit, Abaddon!" Gaap called out.

Abaddon had lost it, though. He picked up the head of the cow, looked it over, and then threw it at his guests. They managed to jump out of the way just in time.

Gaap tried to exit his host and realized that he couldn't! "What have you done?" he questioned Abaddon.

Charlie tried to leave the decrepit old man that he was in about this time, too, and realized that he couldn't. He told Gaap, "I can't get loose from this human host!"

Abaddon laughed maniacally as Gaap glared at him. "You are both stuck in those mortals, you damn traitors, as you deserve! You have dared to side with a human?! They are nothing but pawns in our chess match against God! You treat her as if she is your equal! Yet she is even *gay*! How dare you! We are here, cursed with hideous forms because of them! We suffer because of *them*!"

Abaddon's words shook the walls. He let his own human host fall to the ground in a heap as he rose out of it.

This demon was beyond enraged, and it showed in the form that his green spirit took. He was a seemingly holographic form of a great giant that towered over his guests. He snapped his fingers, and his human host was set on fire instantly, as was the table and food. "This is what we do when we are done using a human, Abby," he thundered down to the mortal. He had the ears of a pig, horns of a goat, and a funny shape to him. He was like an overstuffed sack of flour, with bowl-leggedness and hooved feet. Though it was hard to see the entirety of Abaddon's face, you could make out that he had three deep sockets where eyes would normally go, and they were slanted like those of angry eyes. He had a snout that he gave a great snort out of. He stomped the ground with his hooves, and though his form didn't seem physical, there were great marks in the ground where he had stomped. "I gave you fools my wine, my food, my hospitality, and you spat on it!" Abaddon roared.

Charlie retorted, "You haven't given any of us a chance to explain anything to you!"

The giant bent over and looked Charlie in the eyes. Then he scooped up Gaap in one hand and Charlie in the other. He went and sat across from Abby and barked out, "So, Abby, what is it that these two traitors are so intent on having you explain to me? Choose your words wisely, carpet muncher."

His grip on Charlie and Gaap tightened intensely. Abby saw Charlie's teeth gritting. Even Gaap's human host had grown a shade whiter. Abby opened her mouth and tried to start speaking, but no sound came out. She was speechless.

"Say something, human!" Abaddon roared, his monstrous tone vibrating the floor and walls.

Abby broke out in a rush of words, "There is hope, there is hope for all of us!" But the room grew darker, and the only light now came from the burning man and table.

"What hope is there, bitch?" the demon asked her with a sneer.

Abby heard her new friends crying out in pain and realized that Abaddon had tightened his grip on their hosts even more. "God will save all of us from eternal damnation, if you just give him a chance. If we work together and stop hurting each other, there can be happiness!" Her words echoed throughout the dining hall.

Abaddon laughed. He rang out a harsh reply: "God, save the fallen?! You lie!" There was the sound of bones breaking, and then Charlie cried out in agony.

Gaap shouted out to his old school friend, "It can work, though, Abaddon! What she's talking about makes sense, if you just think about it before reacting!"

Abaddon slammed Gaap down to the ground with great force and held him there. "What does he mean, Abigail?!"

Abby cried out, "God is love! He made us with free will! He knew everything that we would do; everything that you rebel angels have done. He could've simply not made you, if he didn't want you around, and yet he made all of us anyways...knowing what would happen! It's all just his way of teaching us. He cast you out of heaven, like he cast us out of the garden! We fucked up, but it doesn't mean that he won't let us back in. He's just waiting for us to learn from our mistakes! When there is a change, he will let us back in."

Abaddon grew quiet as he thought it all over. But he was stubborn. He didn't want things to change. He liked things the way they were. He boomed out his reply: "I don't change. I like harming others. These two have clearly been around humans too much, and for too long. You, lesbian, you gave them funny ideas! Those ideas don't fly with me, though. This is how it is, and this is how it will stay!"

Gaap gasped out a muffled retort: "Just let her talk to Lucifer himself, then!"

Abaddon lifted him up and slammed him back down to the ground so hard that it knocked him out. Abaddon then explained to Abby and Charlie, "Lucifer will not meet you. Changes will *not* be made. Imbeciles!" He now threw Charlie against a wall so hard that it knocked poor Charlie out too. Abby ran and hid behind one of the dining hall's columns. Abaddon laughed and called out to her, "Aww, does the little human want to play a game of hide-and-seek with me before she dies?" He shrank down to a smaller form. He was still a good seven feet tall, though.

Abby silently pleaded with God to help them get away. Then, she remembered the little bottle of stuff to use against a demon in an emergency! She got it out of the pocket she'd had it in. She waited for Abaddon to find her.

The demon was calling out, "Here, kitty kitty kitty!" Abaddon could sense the beating of her human heart. He jumped around the column that Abby was hiding behind and shouted out playfully, "Boo! Found you!"

Abby chunked the bottle at Abaddon. The glass shattered upon impact with his face, and the dust circled around him. Abby watched in utter relief that this kind of glass could make contact with a spirit. She stared at the bewildered demon as the dust seemed to swallow up his form. What exactly would this dust do? She heard Abaddon let out a scream of anger and defeat. He seemed to be locked in place. "What have you done to me, you bitch?!" the demon roared out. The dust had latched onto his form, solidified it, and kept him frozen in place.

Abby walked over to Abaddon, and circled him in triumph. She looked him over with a smile upon her face as she realized that he was now no more than a sparkling green statue that shouted out insults. She poked at him and tugged at one of his ears, and all he could do was shout out, "Stop it! Stop it right now, woman!" She laughed, said "No," and tugged at his other ear.

"I will incinerate you!" the statue roared. The forms of Charlie and Gaap rose up out of their broken hosts, finally conscious again. They swooped over to where Abby was poking at Abaddon.

Charlie smiled and said to the statue, "You're stuck like that now, buddy." He and Gaap chuckled, and Abaddon roared, "You just wait until Lucifer gets me out of this! You three will suffer like nobody has ever suffered before!"

But Gaap shook his own horned head and replied, "He's not gonna find you anytime soon. I'm gonna send you on a little vacation." He formed a monolith, and told Abby to push the statue into it.

"Don't you touch me, carpet muncher!" Abaddon thundered out.

Abby raised her eyebrows. "Oh, don't touch you? Hmm, I think I'll push you." She gave the statue a great heave-ho into the monolith. It had swallowed up the shouting demon in seconds! The three buddies whooped and hollered, danced around, and even gave each other high fives.

"That was too close!" Gaap exclaimed in great relief.

Abby asked him, "So, were you aware at all what that special dust even does to your kind?"

Gaap stopped the strutting around he was doing and replied, "I mean, no, not really. Lucifer had given it to me once. He'd said to use it on my own kind if they ever go rogue."

Charlie commented, "Knowing Lucifer, it might do something different each time. How much more of that stuff do you have?"

Gaap thought about it. He actually had a good bit back in the angelic weapons room in his fort. Yet how fast would Lucifer find out some of it had been used on Abaddon? All it would take was one minion, one pawn even, to alert the father of chaos. "I have enough of it, but we need to go and grab the rest now!" he replied urgently. But as he was forming another monolith, the doors to the great dining hall opened. Some of Abaddon's guards entered with another.

The main guard announced, "My lord, Pavlov is here to see you. He said that it couldn't wait until after your dinner."

Of course, the new arrivals noticed the scene in front of them. Abaddon was nowhere in the room, for starters. Pavlov's icy eyes locked in on the most unusual sight he'd ever seen: a girl with curly red hair following two unknown beings through what seemed to be a hole in the atmosphere! This rip in the atmosphere swallowed them up, and the only thing left in the hall afterward were the fires that had once been a man and a great table. "What is this? Where is my advisor?!" Pavlov asked the bewildered guards.

The legion guards stared at each other in silence as it occurred to them that foul play was afoot. One of them addressed the Russian prime minister. "It just now occurred to me that Abaddon is not here, sir. I must've forgotten what he's currently doing. He is having dinner with an aunt, actually. He is away, in Australia, dining at her place."

Pavlov believed the lie but was very angry with the guards here. He thundered out, "What kind of servants forget where their master is?! This cannot wait!"

The guards circled the prime minister. Their mouths showed no emotion whatsoever. They towered over Pavlov, and one replied, "My apologies. It will have to wait though."

Pavlov barked out, "This is very urgent—do you understand?!"

Another guard thundered back, "It will have to wait."

Pavlov finally seemed to realize how much bigger all these guards were than him. He remembered how cutthroat he'd seen them be to Abaddon's victims of torture before, and he agreed to wait for his advisor to call him. But as he went to the door, he commented to the lot of them, "I will be telling him how I was treated by you lot today. He will surely be firing all of you." He left the dining hall, slamming the doors in a huff.

Once he was gone, the demon guards put the place on lockdown to investigate the dining hall thoroughly. It was no trouble for fallen angels to get a recap on what had previously gone down in a room they were in.

As for the heroes, they had warped right to the room in Gaap's fort that held all that special dust that one could use against demons. "This has gotten pretty dangerous," Abby commented to the other two, as a slight relief passed over her that they were no longer in Abaddon's home. Charlie and Gaap were rushing around, bagging up all the bottles of the demon repellent.

Gaap replied, "It's gonna be much worse if Lucifer reacts the way my old friend just did."

Abby braced herself for more overly large menaces. She asked, "Should I go and get some more clothes?"

The two demons were too distracted loading up dust to realize what a horrible idea that could be. So, Charlie off-handedly replied, "Sure."

Abby headed to the door, opened it, and said, "I'll just find my way there and back then." She scurried off to find the room where she'd been in Gaap's massive fort. She was lost in no time. Looking around her surroundings, she concluded that she was in a greenhouse. There was a nice little koi pond here, surrounded by flowers and greenery the likes of which she'd never seen before. She seemed to be perfectly alone, so she fell to admiring this flower that looked like a posing ballerina and that blossom that looked like a great eye with pink petals all around it. She got closer to the eye flower and commented, "How did God make a flower that can look so much like it's staring at me?"

A rather familiar guard's voice replied to her question from just behind her, "Well, he was the first artist."

Abby whirled around in shock. The guard that she'd actually had very good conversations with was standing there, pointing a spear at her face. Abby stared at him feeling defeated. He asked, "So, where are the other two? Lucifer is beyond furious."

Abby didn't know what to say. "There is nothing to be furious about," she finally said. What had he called himself? "Rahj, I don't know what you've been told, but we are just trying to help everyone."

The guard was surprised that this human had remembered his name, but he kept his spear pointed at her face and replied, "We were told that you lot did something to Abaddon. That is, how do the humans say it...foul play! We have strict orders to catch you three!"

Abby said, "He hasn't been destroyed, if that's what you think. He's just in time-out for now!"

Rahj narrowed his eyes and questioned Abby further. "Where? I hear your kind bleed pretty easily."

Abby prayed for strength. She explained, "Look, we are just trying to get me to Lucifer!"

"Why? So you can do whatever you did to Abaddon to him too?!"

Abby shook her head. "No! I just want to give him a message of hope! I want to tell him that there's still a way that your kind can avoid damnation! Why do you think Charlie and Gaap are helping me? Do you really think that they're stupid or something?"

Rahj was speechless. How he would love a happy ending! Deep down, he always cringed to think of the eternal damnation his kind would face in the long run. It had gnawed at his insides for centuries, and he had always done his best to overlook it. If Abby was right, though, that was worth lowering his spear and siding with her and Charlie and Gaap. Rahj did lower his spear. He said, "Okay, I can get you to where you're trying to go. Afterward, if you lead me to Charlie and Gaap, I can get you all out of here before you're detected by the others. So, where to?"

Abby was shocked. Should she trust him? She didn't really have a choice at this point. "Okay,

Rahj. Can you take me to the room I've been staying in, then?"

Her new comrade gave her a smile. "No problem! It's just a hallway down, really. You were pretty close, little human."

Why did the rebel angels always have to call her that? She responded with an optimistic "Lead the way, Rahj! Oh, but just call me Abby."

"Okay, but I'm going to need you in front of me. It needs to look like you're my prisoner, just in case another guard sees us together. They are all looking for you, Gaap, and Charlie."

Abby agreed and let him point his spear into her back in a menacing manner. "How will I find the room if I'm in front, though?" she asked as he led her to the exit of the greenhouse.

"I'll mutter which way," Rahj assured her. "It's really just taking an immediate right at the end of this hallway." But Rahj was more nervous about running into his own kind than he let on. Demons lying to humans was easy enough, but demons lying to other demons was nearly impossible. They could almost sense when one of their own was being dishonest. Yet Yahweh smiled down on them, apparently happy to have another fallen child of his pick himself up off the ground. The demon guards closest to Abby and Rahj he distracted with random thuds, squeaks, and shadows. Rahj was able to get Abby to her room to gather the stuff she needed with no trouble at all. He even managed to get them both back to where Gaap and Charlie were without being detected!

Now, when Abby first entered the room with Rahj, Charlie and Gaap both panicked. Gaap had been retelling one of his favorite moments as Cupid, and he stopped midsentence and stared at Rahj. Charlie was confused at first but started cussing very fluently when he saw what had made Gaap go speechless. "Abby! What the hell is this shit doing with you?"

Rahj laid his spear on the ground. "I come in peace! I want to help! I can too. Lucifer has everyone looking for you! They say that you've destroyed Abaddon, and they want you dealt with. I am supposed to turn you in if I see you, and yet here I am. Abby has influenced me, and I want to help. You all need to lie low somewhere. But I'm coming too. We need to lie low somewhere the Elite won't think to look and plot our next move there."

Rahj then shed his human guard form. The body fell away from his spirit like a corpse that was not yet dead but not yet awake either. The spirit of Rahj looked just as different as the other spirits that Abby had seen so far. He had a rather skeletal form, with a black color splashed with gold. He wore robes of matching color. He had a fierce appearance, the true marks of one's best guard. He was just as holographic as the others, but he also appeared more majestic than Charlie or Gaap—the guard surpassing his legion commander! Gaap even looked ashamed of himself for a moment there. How funny the world works.

Abby exclaimed, "Whoa! How were you *just* a guard?"

Charlie felt Gaap's wounded pride and commented, "Enough. It's great to have another team player. Where should we go, though?"

They each thought it over. Then three ideas got called out. "Greece!" Gaap said, as Charlie announced his own idea: "Iraq! It's the last place they'd think we'd dare go." Abby had popped in with "The beach! A private beach somewhere warm and not too populated."

Gaap complained, "But beaches are always populated.

Charlie proposed, "How about somewhere in Italy?"

This was agreed upon by all of them. There were a few jokes made about going to Vatican City, but then walls were heard above them being blasted apart. Gaap shouted out, "Okay, okay, We're going to Italy! I have a little spot there. Grab hands!"

CHAPTER 7

The four of them got together and grabbed hands as Gaap formed a monolith. They all went through it just as the door to the room they were in was blasted off its hinges. He had stored all the demon dust that they'd bagged up in his own little storage monolith, so they weren't leaving empty handed either.

From the monolith they'd disappeared through, they stepped out onto what was known as Alicudi Island, a remote island near Sicily. It was around two in the morning here, so hardly a soul stirred. They had stepped into a white bricked home that stretched out a good ways. Abby walked to the end of the spacious, firelit sitting room they were in now and peered out the blue-curtained opening that led to a balcony overlooking the rocky, boat-filled shores of the island. The view looked just like Abby had always assumed Greece must look. She went out to the balcony and stared at the ocean fondly.

There were countless palm trees here, along with some sort of leaves that climbed up a brick wall that blocked a lovely patio down below from any outsiders. It was opened facing the sand and the waves that crashed to the shore with that fierceness that Abby so loved about the ocean. There was a lit firepit down on the patio with cushioned seats around it. The entire scene looked inviting, but Abby's partners abruptly snapped her out of her daze. As she was gazing at a pentagram-shaped hot tub down there, Charlie called, "Get in here, Abby! Don't draw attention to yourself!"

The human girl snapped back to the ugly reality of their current situation. She hurried back into the quiet sitting room that the others were in. The angels were all seated around a fire in those otherworldly seats. There was a black recliner one of them had set up in this circle that was clearly for a mortal. Abby took a seat in it, but said nothing. Rahj spoke up with the first question: "Okay, so, what now?" He seemed to be the type that was always ready to plan the next move. Perhaps it was the mark of one who had been in a legion since before Abby had even been born.

Gaap answered matter-of-factly, "Well, we're fucked. That's what."

Abby finally spoke. "No. No. We gained another angel! That's a step in the right direction!" She nodded toward Rahj.

Charlie nodded in agreement, but Gaap gave a sigh and said, "Yet everyone is looking for us! We can't go anywhere!"

Charlie argued back, "We just did! We came here!"

Abby and Rahj nodded.

Gaap felt nervous, though—helpless, really. "Everyone is against us!" he moaned, feeling defeated.

Rahj spoke up to his old commander: "God isn't." The fire in the fireplace grew brighter at these words.

This brought Gaap a sense of comfort. He understood for the first time that there was nothing to fear with the creator himself smiling down on him again. He came up with something then. "Okay, okay, I see the bigger picture, really. Hiding will do us no good. Let's just get it over with. Let's go to Lucifer!"

The others got nervous now, though. Rahj replied, "That's pretty extreme." Charlie added, "He is more powerful than any of us!"

But Gaap retorted, "Okay, so? Yahweh is more powerful than him, is he not?"

Abby spoke up. "It's scary. It's terrifying, even. I don't think it's going to be in any of our mental comfort zones, but isn't this the whole point? Stand up to Lucifer and ask him to put aside his animosity with God…? We are just the messengers!"

Charlie sighed and stared into the dancing flames. The flames gave him an encouraging smile! Charlie smiled back. He said to the group, "We should go to the Vatican. We could appear in the hidden room that they keep the Ark of the Covenant in. The Elite would be there in five minutes tops. They would either bring Lucifer to us, or us to him."

Rahj nodded in agreement. "Okay, so let's bring anything we feel may be helpful, I say."

"I'm the human!" Abby said. "So, I should find a good outfit—you know, good running shoes, flexible pants with good pockets, shit like that." The fallen angels chuckled as the fire warmed Abby's cheeks but did nothing for her nerves.

Charlie replied to her, "Go ahead, then."

Gaap added, "Yes, Abigail. Go and find what you can wear to stand up against one with the face of a clock, the impenetrable body of a robotic dragon, and the force of all of your world's militaries combined."

"I wish you luck, little human," Rahj said.

Abby gazed open mouthed at the others as she pictured this description of Satan's true form for the first time ever. What physical attire would prepare any human for that? Yet the mortal girl knew there was no turning back. She asked them where her outfit choices would be.

Gaap replied, "Second room on the left, down that hallway."

Abby thanked him and went to explore her options. As she looked over bulletproof vests that would match anything, pants that could get her from point A to point B without making her feel fat, and cute shoes that she could run in, she realized that the appearance simply didn't matter. One fully geared mortal girl was *nothing* against the face of time with functions that would make a dictator cower. God was the only one that could knock Chaos off his feet. She herself was just the tool—just a messenger spreading hope to the hopeless.

Abby returned to her crew in all-black attire and shoes. She wore her curls up where they would be out of the way and had little bottles of that demon repellent in her pockets. Gaap applauded, and exclaimed, "That's kickass! I have just the thing to add! Just in case there are some humans in the mix that get out of hand."

Rahj chimed in, "Abby seems to be the hands-on type. Let me give her something instead. I have a scimitar and holster for it that you can loop around your hips. Here."

So, after a demonic weapon makeover from Gaap and Rahj, with Charlie watching in amusement in the background, Abby was ready to go. Her signature knuckles was always in one pocket too.

In the meantime, Marie and Lucifer's other minions were going berserk trying to locate the traitors for their king. Pavlov had finally been alerted as to why Abaddon hadn't been at his home the other evening, and he was livid that foul play had been brought on upon his advisor and best friend, Abaddon. He was out for blood. The Elite's latest meeting went above and beyond terrible in sacrifices to their king. They all sat and watched a group of alligators devour an entire family of the most impoverished people. Then, they drank the blood of the oldest and youngest victims in the family, and Marie spoke in solemn tones: "We do this for you, our king of all that is chaos. Help us to help you." Glasses clanked, the members drank, and everyone said in unison, "So mote it be."

Afterward, Pavlov was the first to speak. "I know that information is being withheld from me about my advisor! Marie, what are you not telling me? I do not like secrets. I feel I am being made a fool of. I have brought Ukraine to its knees for this group! I have slaughtered many, and drunk the blood of countless for a king that I never see! I want, no...I *demand* answers!" He pounded the table with his fist at the end of his rant.

Marie narrowed her eyes as some of the other wealthy pansies in the room muttered their agreements. She retorted, "We don't care if Russia gains Ukraine, you foolish little man! Need I remind you that it is just to distract the public and scare them into compliance for whatever move their supposed country is making next?! We make them think what *we* want! We make them want, and like, what benefits *us*! Get over the country you are a mere mascot for, and join the reason that I have called this meeting today! It concerns your dear advisor anyways! Abaddon is MIA! He was one of our main agents, not just the lapdog of Pavlov here."

She was speaking to the entire group now. "We are looking for the perpetrators as we speak. There seem to be three of them involved. One is just a girl that can be easily dealt with. The other two are much more dangerous. Normal weapons will not work on them."

The other members of the Elite looked dumbfounded, scared, and curious.

Marie continued: "Your drivers that bring you here, as you know, our king handpicked them himself. This is due to them not being entirely human."

There were excited murmurs, interrupted by Pavlov's next outburst. "*Where* is Abaddon?!" He slammed his fist on the table again.

Marie glared at the Russian stooge and barked out, "We do not know! He isn't dead, though, so just shut up!"

Yet Pavlov interjected, "How could you know that he isn't dead, if you don't know where he is?"

Marie explained, "Because he, also, isn't human! Just like everyone here's personal driver, and like the two men we are looking for that travel with the mortal that stirred this shit up, Abaddon is alien. These...aliens...were booted out of their own kingdom by a great big bully, and they came here and have been helping us in secret for ages. They helped build pyramids and temples, they taught us of medicine and good hygiene, and they even introduced us to weapons. Their leader goes by the name of Lucifer, the ones that help us. He is our king, and we owe him everything."

There were murmurs all across the table now as everyone took this information in. There was a vague memory of hearing his soothing, melodious tones in a previous meeting, but the king had messed with his forces' memories a few times for his own advantage. Marie gave them a minute to talk this over, and then added, "He prefers to go by the name of Chaos now."

A Swedish man who was a very well-known CEO asked Marie, "So, where is he?"

There were murmured agreements to this, until a male voice spoke from the shadows of the room. "I am right here, my dearest mortal friends," The silhouette of a tall and handsome man emerged. He had a relatively nice and athletic build. He had piercing blueish-silver eyes, well-kept short blond hair, and a nice tan. His shoes were so shiny that you could see yourself in them. As for his tailored black business suit and black tie, they looked like they cost as much as a Porsche! He bore the expression of one that would take nobody's shit, and yet he was so charming that you longed for his approval. He spoke more as he maneuvered gracefully into the room. His voice was so musical, you felt like you were being serenaded.

Lucifer sat down next to Marie and then spoke to the group in more earnest. "You have done well for me and my kind. It goes appreciated. Yet, I have been betrayed by two of my own. The two that travel with some mortal girl. The ones who have betrayed me are very tough. They are also, as of now, the enemy."

Pavlov asked Lucifer, "So, Abaddon is one of you?"

Chaos gave his puppet a solemn nod.

Pavlov inquired further, "So, what exactly are you, then? You look pretty human to me. So did Abaddon."

Chaos replied softly, "I am much more than human. You mortals see so little. Your kind's vision is just so limited."

The Chinese dictator asked the king, "Your Majesty, how will we know what exactly we are looking for if these two traitors happen to be in their natural form?"

Chaos gave him a look over before answering. "I will give you all a glimpse of our true forms," He stood up, clapped his hands, and called out,

"Drivers! Come in here and shed your skins for my mortals of the future."

The Elite watched their own drivers fill the room. They watched in amazement as the drivers rose up out of their mortal hosts and hovered in the air as their mortal "suits" fell to the floor in unconscious heaps. The wealthy members of the Elite looked over their holographic demons. Some had the horns of rams, others had hooved feet, and some had the heads of jackals or hawks. They were glorious to behold save for the one flaw in appearance that each was cursed with. The demons soaked up the awe that they knew their humans were feeling. Lucifer let them bask in it for a moment as human and demon stared at each other with an acceptance that the demons rarely got. Then one mortal called out to their king, asking him, "What do you look like then?"

Lucifer stared into the man's very soul before replying. "None of you are ready to behold my true form just yet. Someday, you all will see it, but now is not the time." The demons that hovered around all chuckled at this, for they knew the form that their king spoke of.

Lucifer addressed his fallen comrades, "That's enough for now. Thank you, my kin." The fallen angels collected their hosts and left the room. Chaos said to his human pawns now, "I need you all to simply focus on finding the three that took Abaddon."

One woman asked him, "How will we detain one of your own, though?"

Chaos replied, "I am going to arm your finest with a special dust that is used for my own kind if they go rogue. It keeps them in line if they choose such behavior as these two have." So it would go down like that. Lucifer, who had betrayed his own father, felt the stab of betrayal too, now—by his standards, anyways. He was a wonderful angel, mind you. Yet when his other self clouded his judgment and Satan came out, Chaos ruled all in his mind. His pride had been wounded, and he deceived his supporters and told them to lie and deceive the masses. He told them to lie and alert the public that Abby, Charlie, and Gaap were the most dangerous and maniacal terrorists of the century.

"We are going to alert every country's media outlets that these three are terrorists of the worst kind and that they want the world to burn. I want the world thinking that they are more of a threat than Pavlov himself!"

King Chaos had a headache in this human form, due to the stress of this whole situation. He looked over at Pavlov and added, "Do you want to save your advisor friend? You are going to make a public announcement that you are going to back off from your pursuit of Ukraine long enough to help find these three."

Pavlov stammered out, "I-I-I...you...want me to stop fucking with Ukraine?"

The devil gave the Russian prime minister a look so chilling, so full of an inhuman rage, that the Russian quickly agreed and said no more.

"Find them," Chaos ordered the group. "Have the ones that I approve of use the dust that I will supply your forces with, but only if need be. I want them brought to me, alive."

Lucifer got up, made to walk to the door, but then simply vanished instead. The room of world leaders, pharmaceutical owners, CEOs, and producers all looked Marie's way. Nobody spoke at first. Finally, the woman realized that it was up to her to break the ice. "Fox, CNN, BBC, spread the word. Every news source out there is to be alerted that there are very harmful terrorists on the loose. They have infiltrated my satellites and are aiming nukes at *each* country! They *must* be found at once!"

Everyone stood up and began hustling out. One of the best screenwriters wrote Pavlov a script to read in front of the cameras. The Elite got ready to take down these traitors, but thankfully, not a one of them knew that there were actually four of them, not three. Nobody yet knew that another rebel had joined their ranks.

Rahj was still unknown to most, being a mere legion demon and all. If the crew of rebels played their cards right, his presence could go unnoticed for a while. So, the next evening, when the report came on the news regarding "the three most-wanted terrorists," the four rebels laughed in good spirits. They all sat, relaxing, around the TV as Charlie remarked, "This gives us an advantage! If everyone is looking for three of us, and we have four, we just need good disguises long enough to get into the Vatican!"

Rahj asked, "Why would we bother with disguises if we're popping up where the Ark of the Covenant is if we're trying to draw Lucifer to us?"

Charlie shrugged and said, "Precaution."

Abby brought up an idea now. "What if Rahj stays hidden in there with some of the dust, and we can get a better advantage at getting Lucifer there alone to talk?"

Gaap nodded. "That could even give us an escape route in case things don't work out. I mean, who says that he would actually be the one to come after us himself if it's that random?"

There were murmured agreements around the room. Abby added another thought: "Maybe I could record some things with my phone and get out what is really going on in the Vatican."

Charlie wasn't sure about that, though. He replied, "I don't know if you should go that far. This group runs the internet too. They would take your findings down from social media as soon as one of their pawns saw it."

"Unless we keep them from doing that," Rahj argued. "We could dust anyone that notices the phone."

Gaap sighed. "Do you even know what the dust does to our kind?"

Rahj replied, "I know that it can't kill us."

"But it's only been used once!" Gaap said. "For all you or me know, it could do different things each time! Maybe there is a way it *can* destroy one of us randomly."

Rahj shook his head and retorted, "It can't kill one that can't die!"

As the two argued about this, Abby and Charlie shouted out, "Shut up!" Gaap and Rahj went quiet, both feeling slightly heated.

Charlie sighed and looked over at the human he'd come to respect. He asked her, "Do you want to try and expose what the Elite have done to this world as we try and talk to Lucifer?" Abby gave a determined nod. Charlie and Gaap looked at each other and then at Rahj. Charlie then said, "Everything we're doing is risky. So, I say what's one more risk? I'm down to try this too."

There was mutual agreement from Rahj and Gaap to this, and the four rebels readied themselves for the main event. They had gotten everything together and been ready earlier, really, but then decided to relax with the news on and wait it out. Now that they knew they were all over the news, there was no more time to waste.

CHAPTER 8

Once the last preparations were made, they all gathered together, Gaap formed a monolith, and they grouped hands and went through that big old hole in the atmosphere. They stepped out into one of the Vatican's secret candlelit rooms, which was stocked with hidden documents, books, paintings, and other treasures. They had Rahj duck down behind some piles of golden coins and jewels, with some of the special dust. He was to remain hidden there until things seemed out of hand.

The other three began walking down a slated path, with Abby's footsteps making the only sound. The Ark of the Covenant was certainly here, in this very room. They could see it a ways up ahead! It sat atop some stone steps at the end of the path. The candlelight being the only source of light in here, it gave the ark a mystical aura. It looked like a little kitchen island made of gold, with two angelic figurines praying atop it. Abby stared at the golden wings of the figurines in awe. On each side of the ark were two golden carrying handles as well, clearly used to get it from point A to point B.

Abby was so overcome with the urge to see the ancient artifact up close, and maybe even see what it would feel like to touch it, that she began sprinting up to it. Charlie and Gaap and even Rahj swooped over to her and blocked her path at once. Angels, fallen or not, were very fast. "What are you thinking, Abigail?! No human can touch that without many special rituals first! You would fall dead immediately!" Charlie shouted angrily. The other two demons nodded in earnest, staring at Abby in disapproval.

Abby gazed at the artifact behind them and replied, "I know, I've heard. I just…I just thought that that was only the rule for it back in ancient times. I just wanted to see what something that legendary and that old feels like. Clearly someone got it in here without dying."

Gaap retorted, "Foolish girl, you think humans did? That's like saying Solomon had only humans build his temple!"

Abby knew that he'd made a valid point, so she peeled her eyes off the ancient artifact and focused on her rebel posse. "Is that what your kind looked like before the fall?" she asked the spirits.

Rahj muttered, "I'm going back to my hiding spot." He floated off in a huff.

Abby frowned and asked the other two, "Should I not bring up the fall?"

"Don't worry about it right now," Gaap said. But he added, "We weren't solid golden winged beings either. Most of us weren't, anyways. We have different hues to our own forms."

Charlie remarked, "We *did* have wings."

Gaap nodded and said, "But our wings all looked different. Some had two wings; others had six. Some even had eyes throughout their wings."

Charlie gazed off into space and added, "The most majestic and beautiful wings, though...the most artistic wings...they belonged to God's favorite angel."

A chilling male voice spoke from just behind them now: "Lucifer's wings themselves."

The three whirled around in great shock. Floating a little ways off the ground were three spirits that looked like ancient Egyptian gods. One that looked like Seth had spoken. He glared at Gaap and Charlie and then said, "You disgust me."

Gaap couldn't find his voice, so bad were his nerves at this moment. Charlie said, "You don't know the whole story."

Seth shouted back, "You were an outcast anyways! But Gaap, how could you?!"

Abby found her own voice now. "Are you going to just talk shit, or are you going to take us to Lucifer?"

The other demons stared at this tiny lady with mixed expressions. At least one stared at her in fascination that she'd even had the guts to speak. The others glared at her in hatred, though. Seth spoke to her: "What makes you think that we are taking you? He could be coming here. He could even have requested that we simply kill you.

Maybe he even wants us to throw some of our own human pawns in here to rape you for a while, eat one of your arms, and knock down that confidence of yours."

His cohorts snickered unpleasantly. But Abby held in her terror. She looked Seth in the face and retorted, "I am not afraid."

"You will be," Seth said. He let those words sink in before he spoke again. "He will be coming here, actually."

Charlie piped in again. "Has he even been alerted that we're in here?"

The sarcasm in his question enraged Seth further. He snarled at Charlie and then fired back. "No, but I will be taking care of that in due time."

This was the very response that the rebels had hoped for. Charlie had remembered in their schooling that Seth had never been too good about thinking before speaking. Right on cue, a cloud of dust enveloped the lot of them! Charlie and Gaap had gotten out of the way just in time, for they'd known it was coming. Rahj gave them a smile and a nod from where the demon guards had been previously. Abby was so relieved, as were the other two. The other demons, the ones caught by the dust, had slowed down dramatically, until they simply couldn't move anymore. They were suspended in motion. Gaap then sent each one into their own *time-out* through a monolith.

Abby now asked her rebel spirits, "So, should we just wait here for Lucifer?"

Rahj shook his head. "I don't know, Abby. With that ark there, I'm afraid that you might just get too tempted to try and touch it again."

Gaap nodded and added, "Lucifer could get you to think that you should just go ahead and touch it for all sorts of bullshit reasons."

Charlie asked Abby, "Did you get anything juicy for social media?"

Abby had forgotten about her phone. As she started digging around in her pockets, she realized that it wasn't even there! Could she have dropped it during the ordeal they'd just gone through? "I can't find my phone!" she replied.

She and her spirits started retracing their steps. But after looking all over the path they'd gone down, they eventually gave it up as a lost cause.

"There's no telling where your phone ended up. You might not have even brought it. Let's just...

improvise," Gaap commented. The others looked over at him in wonder. So he explained further, "Lucifer wants to find us at this point, right?" The others nodded, and Gaap continued, "So, we have access to get to him now through one of my monoliths!"

Abby asked, "How do we expose the Elite's schemes, though?"

Gaap shrugged. "Let's just see what happens. How do you mortals word it, ah yes! Let's play it by ear!"

They all thought this over. Rahj commented, "It's better than keeping this game of cat and mouse up," and the others agreed.

Gaap formed a monolith, and they all held hands and went through that hole that Abby was getting so used to. The rebels stepped out onto white marble floors with exquisite rugs positioned here and there. Columns lined a grand hall with cacti and art that had a western feel to it. The furniture in the center of this spacious room was made of oak and had cushions of the same blues as the room's rugs. There was a shiny black sculpture nearby that looked like the silhouette of a cowboy tilting his hat. There was a great sky lift right above where the furniture was all positioned. It boasted a starry nighttime sky at the moment. A dancing glow of light came from a roaring fire in a grand fireplace facing the seating area.

The four rebels grouped together and but hadn't yet uttered a word to each other before Lucifer's voice rang out in melodious tones: "My own kind have come to betray me and all I stand for, with a human...a lesbian, at that. Well, here I sit. Come and face me."

He was in a human form, for the moment. Since he was the morning star, he could change this at will and didn't even need a host most of the time. He boasted the sculpted form of a man that never missed a workout, or a shower for that matter. He was so well groomed, with curly locks the color of honey today. One moment his eyes were a piercing blue, and the next, they could be a deep maroon. Perhaps, with feelings of betrayal, his eyes were showing a hint of the power within him.

The rebels slowly approached Satan, and the fallen star casually said, "Come and have a seat. Don't you three give me that 'but I'm a spirit' garbage either. The furniture here is designed to seat mortal and angel alike. We will all seat together as equals." So the four of them sat around Lucifer quietly. He looked them over, and said, "Four of you...here I had thought that only two of my own had betrayed me."

Abby spoke, her voice shaking slightly: "None of them have done anything that betrays you, great Morning Star. They just wanted to help me get to you, so I could speak with you, face to face."

Lucifer pondered her words with a grim expression. Then he replied, "How is it that you think you can lie to the ultimate deceiver himself? You may be a reasonable little actress, but I am not a fool, Abigail. It is mutiny that these three are committing. How many of your own have you used the forbidden dust on now? Gaap, you have betrayed me the most." He then added, "I would expect this sort of thing from the two no-names, but you, Gaap...why?"

Cupid gazed into the eyes of his mentor, eyes that were now a beautiful shade of amber. He could feel the hurt within them, and yet he could see the pride overriding so many other emotions that kept the great dragon in balance. Gaap was very careful with his response. He did not want that dragon nestled around Lucifer's pupils out. "My King, I want what we all want. None of our kind will admit this, but we all *do* want to be okay in the end. Abby here, she believes that there is still a chance for our kind, Lucifer."

Charlie spoke up now, adding, "We think Father will forgive us if we just ask him to. The fallen that got dusted, they're just in holding cells of sorts. They haven't been destroyed."

Yet Lucifer was overcome by anger, and it was slowly building up. His eyes were violet now.

He said to Charlie, "You fall for the lies of a mortal, about a father that cast us down here for a stroke of rebellion...we grow closer to our doom, and you would leave us in the dust."

Abby felt like things weren't going very well, so, she interjected, "I'm just trying to give your kind some hope, a way out of the impending doom that you all think is coming your way."

Lucifer stood up, revealing just how tall and sculpted he really was in his human form today. He walked over to the fireplace and put his hands in the reddish flames. Abby watched in shock as she saw how satisfied he looked at placing his hands in fire! Lucifer drew his hands back out of these flames, and there was absolutely no damage to them whatsoever!

The great and ancient creature spoke to them. "You know, I don't much prefer the name Lucifer anymore. I rather like the name of my favorite word: Chaos...yes...King Chaos...it has a nice ring to it."

Rahj now spoke. "I know how you feel, sir. Don't let your pride and anger get in the way of a way back home, though. You know you were our father's favorite!"

Yet Chaos emitted a red glow around his physical persona now. The others in the room felt a change in the atmosphere. Even in the portraits along the walls, the stallions suddenly looked outraged. The chandeliers above were made all of antlers, but now there were hissing cobras coiled around them. Where there had been the sound of cheery fiddles playing in the background before, the rhythm had changed to the chilling sounds of violins and a piano playing a very ominous tune indeed. "I *was* his favorite. Yet then *they* came along," Lucifer grumbled, nodding over at Abby. He added, "Father wanted us to bow to the likes of them. He had all of these rules and regulations that came with them too."

Abby asked, "What makes you think you aren't still his favorite?"

But Lucifer laughed at that and went back to warming his hands in the dancing flames. He turned and looked at Abby as he continued to warm his hands. "I was too rebellious for *Father dearest.*"

Abby argued back. "Maybe you're the reason they tell that one parable—maybe you're his prodigal son! Think about it. You've got the law-abiding angels and humans who have barely ever put a toe into the great oceans of free will, and yet you also have the rest of us: the ones that plunge into the waves of thinking for ourselves! He has his robots, but then he has his misfits who plunge into the waters of experiencing cause and effect! You don't think he admires the ones that actually use the mind he gave them? You really think he isn't proud when our mistakes sting like a jellyfish and we move on, letting it be a lesson learned? Come on! He knew who would be a rebel before he made any of us. Yet he made us anyways. A truly *loving* God wouldn't make someone that wouldn't come back to him one day! A loving God wouldn't make one that would eventually spend eternity suffering!"

Lucifer heard Abby's words, and they had an impact on him for sure. How he longed for this to be true. Yet, humanity itself had pegged him as *the great evil* that would be destroyed someday. Barely anyone had bothered to hear his side of the story. He barked out to Gaap, "So this is what you're hoping for?! You think that *Yahweh* will embrace you and these other two traitors for casting me aside and coming back to him holding white flags?!"

Charlie retorted, "Well, why not? Eternity is eternal. Perhaps he *did* cast us down here to simply learn how to master free will...how to master coexisting, even! If we can do that, maybe we really can go back!"

Rahj threw in a cheery, "Maybe we could even get our wings back." There were nods of agreement from the others.

Lucifer turned and faced them. He thundered out, "That is not how it has been written!"

Gaap barked back, "Words of the beginning civilizations—*for* the beginning civilizations—tampered with throughout history by human and angel alike just to keep certain rulers in power and fear controlling the masses! We tampered with seventy percent of it at least! We damned *ourselves* through lies that *we* influenced the humans to write!"

Lucifer shook his head. "Our sons were coined giants by them. They have been damned to the underworld itself. They are still there *today!* Our *father* did that!"

Abby replied, "Well, maybe they're just there until you lay down your sword."

Lucifer thundered back, "I don't use a sword! You don't even know what you're talking about, *human*!" He added, "You were not there the day that he cast us out! You were not there the day he flooded the world and drowned most of our children!"

Abby shouted, "So tell me about it! Tell me what happened. Tell me what *really* happened!"

Lucifer decided that it might be nice to rant. He spoke in a calmer manner now. Calling out to the walls themselves, he said, "Mercury!" A spot of the wall bulged out to form the shape of a pale blue spirit who wore ancient Greek attire and winged sandals. As he withdrew himself from the wall completely, the wall looked as normal as it had before.

Mercury swooped over to Chaos in a whirl of blue mist, gave him a small bow, and asked, "You called, My King?"

Lucifer nodded and said to the demonic Hermes, "I need you to get the word out to all of my followers, spirit and human alike, that I am not to be disturbed right now."

Mercury gave Lucifer a professional salute. "Affirmative, Your Majesty!" He swooped away, back into the wall without a single glance at the others.

King Chaos said to his guests, "I will need you to stand up while I get the atmosphere just right for this story."

Abby and the others got up, and waited for Lucifer to get the area the way he felt it should be for a recap of what had made Lucifer change to the path of Chaos. Everything went dark. The fire in the fireplace had even gone out! A few seconds later, though, the light of another fire emerged. These flames came from a bonfire. There were cushions situated around this bonfire: some were black, and others were blue. In the background, there were cedar trees, bushes, overturned logs, and even mushrooms and fallen leaves that dotted the ground. There were the sounds of cicadas and the occasional bird now, and it made Abby wonder if they were somehow outside somewhere. Even the ceiling seemed to have transformed into actual sky, with stars dotted throughout it and a crescent moon overhead.

Abby and the others sat on the cushions that were placed around the great big bonfire and waited for Lucifer to begin his story. The devil sat on a black cushion on top of a tree stump that faced his audience and began his story, "For a time, heaven was perfect. We would all just do whatever we wanted. We swam, we flew, we raced each other from one galaxy to the next. I made music, I taught my kin to harmonize, and then I introduced more variety in rhythm by making different kinds of instruments. There was laughter, friendship, competitions, and even pranks. After a while, though, we grew bored of what eventually became the same old songs, games, and same old routines. We craved something new. We wanted adventure! So, Yahweh came up with the idea to make another galaxy with a different kind of world. He decided to make a planet that had greenery unchecked, beaches scattered here and there, and a new kind of being. He made animals like it was nothing. There were different ones that would evolve into bigger and better kinds of themselves. It was a very exciting moment. He then told us that we would have dominion over them.

"But then...he made the humans. We took a back seat while suddenly *Adam* was naming each animal. We watched from the background now, as *your* kind got the luxuries that *we* were promised! Father expected us to just get over it and sing. When the female humans came along, though, me and some other angels had our way with them. We offered them the knowledge of good and evil. We rebelled and purposely tainted them. Father cast us out of heaven...for using the free will that he gave us to use. How does one give you the ability to choose how to live your life and then damn you for doing so?"

Abby replied in a voice of pity, "How indeed."

But Lucifer wasn't giving her the chance to continue. He just rambled on: "Our children were punished for our doings. We created life with human women, and I guess because *Father* hadn't created them, it suddenly wasn't okay! Ask the one these traitors want to run back to where our children are now! I am *fed up* with Father and his self-righteous haters that claim to be loving! Yahweh and his puppets have made me out to be the bad guy, and now I will be! Allow me to show you all *true* Chaos! I will give you reason to hate me." He was looking less human by the minute now.

Abby got ready to throw some of that special dust at him if she needed to. But would that stuff work on the devil himself? Lucifer glared at his own and thundered out, "I will not bargain with traitors. I am going to rip your spirits to shreds and scatter them all over the place!" King Chaos levitated into the air and shed his human form like a snake shedding its skin. He rose up higher into the air in a dark, shadowy form that seemed to be forming into something else entirely. The others got up from their cushions and backed away.

As Satan's shadow began to expand midair, it took the form of a great black dragon with golden ancient runes etched into his massive and robotic form. The horns atop his head of terror looked so sharp that they could most likely cut through steel! Abby chunked a little bottle of the special dust up at him. Though it hit him, nothing happened. Satan laughed, and spoke in a more menacing boom of a voice now, his words reverberating throughout the enchanted room. He stretched his massive mechanical form out in a prideful and taunting manner. He looked down at Abby and said, "I made that dust! I made it to keep my own kind in check! I am immune to what it does, you silly little mortal. I will gladly demonstrate its function on *who* it was meant for, though!"

King Chaos bore a clock for a face. Though he did have sharp black horns above his dragonish ears, and though his face was shaped like that of a great and terrible dragon, within was a dreadful black-and-golden clock etched with Roman numerals. This clock was even up to date with what time it really was! One of the taunting hands on it was counting down the seconds even. It was so like Chaos to want you constantly on edge.

Abby had never had enough time for anything her whole life, kind of like the rest of us. Time is never a friend to humans. Gaap was ready to retreat. He was forming a monolith at once. He beckoned for the others to hurry over to him and grab his hands. But he and his freshly formed monolith were what Chaos shot for with an emerald-green dust in the blink of an eye. The dust had come from the mouth of the great dragon. Imagine seeing the face of a clock form a mouth suddenly and shoot that strange alien dust at one of your newest friends! Abby found herself in a whirlwind of one too many emotions at this point. She was rooted to the spot as she watched that dust engulf Gaap.

Charlie and Rahj stopped running toward Gaap as the dust engulfed him. It reshaped their buddy into the form of a screaming baby and then pushed him through the monolith he'd formed. The monolith then disappeared, and the others panicked.

Chaos laughed and asked his guests, "Who is next? I will each other you separately in your own dungeon and torment you in the way that I find to be best."

Abby tried to sound brave. "Please, just stop! Let it all go! Lay down your weapons, lose your pride! Let go of that anger, Lucifer!"

Satan wasn't going for it, though. He replied, "Ummmm, no. I do grow tired of your false hopes, Abigail." He flew over her and circled around her like a vulture. He said, "While I mindfuck *your* kind to hate and harm those that are *not* like them, I also play *God*! I have pretty much replaced the father who turned his back on me! He will not have a world to save if I devour it after making you mortals no better than me!"

Charlie shouted out to Chaos now, "If you would just apologize and own up to your own mistakes, he would let you back in!" Yet the response he got from the great dragon was a deafening roar. It shook the ground that Abby stood on, even as Satan said playfully to her, "You seem to really care about the animals, Abigail. Have I got a treat for you! I have a few *starving* lions that would love you to feed them."

Abby had nowhere to run from what she could tell was coming. She had no way to fight a mechanical dragon that held the strength of all the militaries in the world. All she could do at this point was put her trust in God.

"Would you like to know what you'll be feeding them? Why, you yourself will have the honor of getting chomped up by your dearest dream pet!" King Chaos was telling Abby. He had done his research on her enough to give her the most ironic death possible. He called out to someone in a very alien language. A pair of doors opened on their own, and some emaciated lions ran through. They pelted toward Abby as if they knew that it was she the great dragon wished them to go for. They had just gotten their postures ready to pounce, when Charlie and Rahj got their angelic wings back!

The two newly restored angels shot toward the lions and bashed them in their sides with their fierce and intimidating wings! You see, the wings of an angel are beautiful, sure, but they're also very powerful weapons. That's not widely known among humans, of course. Abby was one of the only humans to realize this, as she watched the impact of the blow knock the lions through the walls that had come back during the craziness. These lions did not return.

"How the *fuck* did you get your wings back?!" Satan thundered out in a rage. He zeroed in on Abby. He blew fire from his mouth now. Yet Charlie and Rahj swooped over there and shielded her from the flames with their wings—wings of a bedazzling gold for Rahj and a sparkly black for Charlie. The wings were massive! Abby could feel heat from Satan's flames as they made impact with her friends winged shields. Chaos engulfed the trio in flames hotter than we can imagine. He didn't even stop for a full six minutes! Yet as the flames stopped and the smoke cleared, Chaos saw that Abby, Charlie, and Rahj seemed to be just fine! Rahj's and Charlie's wings didn't seemed damaged in the least either!

Again, King Chaos let out a roar of rage. Some of his best demon-kin entered the room now, despite Mercury's message earlier. They were concerned due to the sounds of their king's rage. They kept their distance upon entering the enchanted room, though, knowing that if Lucifer was in his true dragon form, he would not want them to help unless he requested it. They stood on the other side of the room, hovering slightly above the ground and watching the scenario unfold. One of the spirits, who looked like a bride whose heart had been crushed too soon, pointed over to Charlie, and uttered, "Is that *Charlie*?!" She was asking the spirit next to her.

The other spirit replied, “It is! How did he and that other one earn their wings back?!”

A voice thundered over all of them, saying, “Rumel and Rahj have both been pardoned for their rebellions of the past. They embraced their enemy and united to try and open your own eyes to a very simple truth. There is a way back to me, for each and every one of you: human and demon alike. Whether or not you’re ready to lay down your animosities, your cruelties to each other, and your jealousies, that is up to each and every one of you.”

At first, everyone was too shocked to speak. King Chaos was the first to speak, of course. He gave God a grumbling, “Well, why don’t you show yourself then?”

There was a moment’s silence, followed by Yahweh’s reply. “Come now, Lucifer. You just want to fight me. Have you forgotten that I am omnipotent?”

Chaos retorted, “Yeah, yeah, yeah! You’re omni-everything! Why don’t you face me like a *god* then?!”

The demons across from the others all jeered and hissed at God. One of them even shouted out,

"Come on down here, you deadbeat dad!" But the demons whimpered and knelt to their knees as soon as a blinding white light appeared next to the devil.

Abby couldn't look at this strange and overly bright light at all! The glare from it alone caused her to have to simply look at the ground. She, Charlie, and Rahj dropped into the same kneeling position that the demons had dropped to in their own fear.

One of the demons cried out, "Forgive me, Father, please!" Yahweh replied with a nod that only the angels and demons could see. He said to the repenting demon, "You are forgiven. Ascend, and be in paradise again."

The spirit that looked like a bride cried out next. "It's that easy? Forgive me too, please! I was too selfish back then! Father, I repent."

Satan watched in outrage as all but one demon asked God for forgiveness. The devil shouted out. "You've lost me a whole group of my own! Fuck you, God!"

His one remaining demon there looked like a Minotaur with a haziness to his brown form. He called out, "D'ah, I'm still here, My King! I will stand with you until I exist no more!"

Yahweh grew in size, and his light formed into that of a great ram. “If you insist, we can duke it out. Your little minion over there, though, he is going to sit this one out,” God explained to Satan and the Minotaur demon.

The Minotaur argued back, “I’m not going anywhere! You don’t control me!”

To this, Yahweh said, “Actually...”

A small black hole appeared right underneath the Minotaur, sucked the demon down into it, and then disappeared completely. Chaos flipped out completely now, as Abby, Charlie, and Rahj were heard chuckling. He disappeared from view, re-appeared up against the ceiling, and then made a dive for Yahweh. The ram stepped out of the way just in time. A second earlier and Chaos would’ve ripped into him. These two seemed to be made out of the same stuff, yet what that stuff is, I can’t tell you.

Chaos muttered to the ram, “You take my chess piece, I take yours!” He then body-slammed into Abby and her angelic cohorts. They disappeared moments before he would’ve crushed them into physical *and* spiritual dust! God didn’t miss a beat! Chaos looked Yahweh in the eyes. He was one of few beings that could. The ram stared back into the eyes of his hurt child. He knew that what this son of his needed the most at this moment was for the two of them to duke it out. Though he could dust him in an instant, he would give Lucifer what he needed. He said to the fallen angel that he still favored the most, "No chess pieces, my son. It's just you and me."

The atmosphere around them changed completely! There were no walls or ceiling, just a sky that bore suggestions of time being manipulated, as there stretched out all around them the most outstanding sunset—one that looked like something a drunken artist had painted in fits of passionate rage, The scenery around the two ancient beings seemed to be a beach somewhere, but who knew where. The sound of waves crashing into the shore could be heard in the background as God and Chaos circled each other in the forms of a great golden ram and a blackened mechanical dragon with that fearsome clocked face. The ground wasn't sandy, like it would be on a regular beach, though. It was designed like a giant keyboard. As their fight began, each step one of them took played an ominous note. It was as if the two were serenading their own fight!

The great chaotic dragon made a lunge for God with his sharp black-and-gold horns. God let him knock him down, turning the other cheek. Yet he took a minute to get up. Chaos paced back and forth, making the music notes display his impatient irritation. He grumbled, “You aren’t even trying!”

Yahweh slowly got up and asked his prodigal son, “Are you sure you want me to do that?”

Chaos shouted back, “I want you to *burn*!” The great dragon blew fire from his mouth and seemed to roast the ram entirely. He laughed with satisfaction as the flames overtook Yahweh. As this fire continued to burn, though, the ram emerged from the flames.

Before the devil had time to react, God used his ram horns to headbutt Satan with great force. It took that dragon by such surprise that it sent him falling into the depths of the ocean! Satan plunged into the ocean with such a mighty splash that it shook the whole planet! All over the globe, people felt little tremors.

Two friends smoking together in a truck looked at each other all red eyed. One passed the blunt to his buddy while asking, "Dude, did you feel that?"

The other took the blunt, hit it once or twice, and commented, "That was like a little earthquake."

The first replied, "Maybe it's Russia attacking!"

His buddy suggested, "Or the COVID-inspired zombie apocalypse!" They looked at each other fearfully for a few seconds, then laughed, and one said, "Nah, man!" Then they simply went back to peacefully smoking the blunt.

In Russia, the same tremors were felt. One soldier on guard duty somewhere over there said to his battle buddy, "America!" But his buddy shook his head and said, "They are nothing. That was tremor."

Life went on as the fight between the two deities continued. The devil launched out of the waters like an alien missile and shot for the great golden ram! The ram rolled down the keyboard as the dragon slammed down. "This is *my* kingdom!" Chaos screamed out to Yahweh in great fury.

But Yahweh replied calmly, "Only for now, my rebellious son."

The dragon lunged for God, tackled him to the ground, and held him in a choke hold. He thundered out, "When, then? When will it end?!"

Yahweh kicked his son off him with his back two hooved feet. He rose into the air, and an angry dragon followed. So God replied to his son, "When I say so." He gave Chaos a mighty headbutt with his ram horns. It knocked Satan back a bit, but the dragon took hold of the atmosphere in a way that we humans could never do. He saw his father lowering back down to the keyboard, and the sounds of a restful tone were made from his steps.

Lucifer took it up a notch, though, as he came in for a landing. He came snapping at that ram, taking two steps for each one step the ram took. As the two jabbed at each other, dodged, and kicked, the music itself was heard by an artist that just happened to live nearby. The sounds were so inspirational that he wrote his best musical score then and there.

But time seemed to have frozen on the battlefield. Yahweh and Satan were going hard at each other. The great dragon would get frustrated and shoot fire at the golden ram. Then Yahweh would manipulate the flames to form purple butterflies flying by as the flames got near. "You play too much, *Father*!" Satan bellowed as the two now circled each other in the air.

Yahweh tilted his ram head and responded, "Oh, do you grow tired of tricks? I grow tired of your animosity."

Satan spun through the air and jabbed the end of his horned tail into his father's face. He shouted, "Tell me when you are ending this world!"

Yet the ram now grew in size and took the shape of a statue with a face like one of the faces at Stonehenge. He was now so big he could fit the dragon in the palm of his hand. He picked his son up despite the dragon's tail swipe, clawing, and biting. He then sat him back onto the keyboard battlefield. Chaos tried to bite his father's wrist before Yahweh drew away, but God disappeared, saying, "You will know when it is time, son. This fight is over for now."

The angry dragon shouted, cussed, and kicked at the ground, but the ground was sand once more. King Chaos shouted out, "I will bring this world to an end before you do, then!" He formed a monolith and slipped into it, and as it closed up, the beach grew quiet again.

CHAPTER 9

After his fight with God, King Chaos had his members of the Elite spread countless lies about Abby and the angels that had helped her. He even had Pavlov, who had been hated by so many, now looking like a sudden hero! The media was all over some fictitious story about how the Russian dictator had gone *with* some of his best soldiers, pursuing these terrorists across the border. Articles all over the world claimed that Abby and her conspirators had been caught hacking into the satellite systems that Marie owned.

They even had an interview with Marie, who bore a fake black eye. For the cameras, she sobbed as she claimed, "They just burst into my home office one night. They had batons, mace, and even whips! They destroyed countless and irreplaceable vases, statues, and even my chandelier that I'd had the pope himself bless!" She sobbed out the lie so effortlessly that anyone would've believed her. Top-notch eye makeup had been used for that fake black eye; it was completely waterproof.

The camera had zoomed into Marie's destroyed office as she continued: "They wanted codes for my weaponized satellites. When I refused, one of those men—built like Hercules, he was—he punched me in the face and gave me this shiner." The camera zoomed in on the chandelier that was on the floor in many pieces now. "They found *other* codes, though. They have the ability to fire nukes all over the globe, now! They must be found *and* stopped!"

Well, Abby and the others had certainly made front-page news now. Luckily for them, they were currently far away from earth. They had entered heaven itself! Yahweh had the angel at the golden gates let all of them through with no interview needed. He then told them all to go and enjoy paradise for a little while so he could gather some other angels for a meeting that he would be coming and collecting them for in a little while. "For now, just go and do what you love the most," Yahweh told Abby, Charlie, Gaap, and Rahj, and then he simply disappeared in a flash of white light.

The others all looked at each other fondly. "We made a good team," Abby commented to the misfit angels.

Rahj replied, "I would team up with you guys anytime, any day," They all chuckled, relief sweeping over them that they were safe.

Gaap had a golden pitcher and matching flasks appear for each of them. "Let's have a toast to success."

"What's in the pitcher?" Charlie asked.

"Ohh, this is the nectar of the gods, my friends!" Gaap poured a strange golden liquid into each flask and handed them out.

Charlie took his, still not sure what they were about to drink. But what did it matter in heaven? So, he raised his glass with the others, and they all clanked their glasses together, saying a hearty "Cheers!"

They drank the cold, sweet liquor and got instant warm, fuzzy feelings of extra contentment. It wasn't bad at all. Then, Abby noticed something. They all seemed to be made from the same stuff now! She was more spirit than physical, and if that meant what she thought it meant, then she was wasting time hanging around all stationery. The possibilities before her were endless!

As for Gaap, he'd started to simply drink out of the pitcher itself. He commented as he did so, in between gulps, "I can *taste* as a spirit again! This is so good!"

Charlie and Rahj snickered. Charlie then made to grab the pitcher from Gaap, saying, "Ooh, yeah! Give me more then!"

Gaap snatched it away from Charlie, retorting, "Get your own!"

They messed with each other in this manner while Abby decided to try out the new *her* for herself. She wandered down a pastel pathway with purple trees and golden flowers on each side. In the distance, she could hear the welcoming sound of waves crashing up against a shore. She only had to go a little bit farther down the path until she saw a beautiful white sandy beach at the end, with crystal clear blue water. There was a sun in the sky here that gently brought her a wonderful warmth. Abby realized as she caught herself staring at this sunny orb that it wasn't hurting her eyes to look at it!

Grinning ear to ear, Abby stepped off the pastel-colored pathway. She must've suddenly gone shoeless, because she could feel the warm, soft sand at her feet. She donned a sparkly blue dress out of *nothing at all* and headed out into the water. She got into this ocean and knew that she was finally home. She had never felt at home anywhere her entire life! She was riding atop waves now with no board even needed. She could move these waves wherever she wanted, wherever she willed them to go!

There was the sound of drums, flutes, fiddles, a trumpet, saxophones, and even the occasional bagpipe in the background as Abby rode the waves. The melody was upbeat and cheery, with a mixture of reggae and jazz to it. It would get more Celtic here and there, but then it would switch to a grungier beat. She saw Yahweh on the shore after a while, though, and he was calling out for her to come on back for the meeting. It was hard for Abby to make herself get out of the ocean, as it always had been. Yet she knew that this would be important. So she surfed back to the sand and had the wave she was on lower her gracefully onto the shore.

God commented, "Very nice! You aren't too much of a klutz here, I see!"

Abby's cheeks went red even though she lacked physical form now. "It's a nice change," she replied.

Yahweh gave her a warm smile and said, "Well, I'm happy that you approve so far! Come with me for now, though. We need to discuss my most wayward son."

Abby didn't bother to ask who that was. She simply said, "Okay," and walked with God along the pastel-colored pathway.

Today it seemed that Yahweh had decided to take the form of an older Nigerian-type of man with a flowing white beard and dark skin. He looked like somebody that you could just talk about anything with. He led Abby to a lovely green hill with a pond sitting next to it. As they approached the hill, a mouth opened from it, revealing a strange cave! Yahweh held out his hand and said, "Après vous." Abby knew this to be French for "after you." She took his hand and let him help her up into the cave first. She thanked him and then heard some familiar voices up ahead.

Gathered at a very large circular table sat her buddies. They were joined by angels that Abby had never seen before. My, my, how magnificent they looked! Abby longed to take a picture but heard Yahweh's own footsteps and remembered that there was a reason they were all there. "Have a seat anywhere, Abby," Yahweh told her. Abby sat next to Charlie, who was sitting with Rahj and Gaap.

Yahweh went to the head of the table and signaled for the chitchat to die down. Everyone went quiet, and he said to them all, "Hello to all, old and new! All are welcome here! Now, while I would usually hold a celebration to honor new beings here, that will have to wait. Lucifer is being rather...extra...right now. Something will have to be done. I encourage any ideas to be spoken. I do like when my children brainstorm on their own from time to time."

A very masculine angel with an athletic build who was dressed in robes of war spoke up. "I say that we just catch Lucifer, strap him to some of those nukes, and shoot him into space!"

A few of the other angels who wore these same robes muttered agreements. But a smaller faceless silver woman argued, "I just don't think that is how we should deal with him. Lucifer is who made music what it is today!"

Another angel, sporting a red beard, called out, "That doesn't say much!"

Plenty of the Goody Two-Shoes angels laughed at this one, but Abby now spoke up. "Can't we just put him somewhere away from everyone, but *only until* he is ready to change?" All eyes in the cave were on Abby at this suggestion.

"I second this!" Charlie said. "Lucifer is hurting us, but he just needs to see that he can let go and move on. He isn't even Lucifer when he's like this. He's Satan! Well, now he goes by King Chaos, but still...if he was given time...he'd cool off."

Yet another angel slammed his fist down onto the table and argued, "Unacceptable! We have fought—we have been fighting with your lot and him for centuries!"

"And?" Rahj shot back. "We're in here with you now! What makes you think that Lucifer won't change over time? *We* have *eternity*!"

There was murmuring throughout the cave now. Some agreed, and others did not. Abby looked over at Yahweh and asked, "Isn't there a way for all of us in the long run?" The room went quiet.

All looked to God, and he beamed at the one human there. He replied, "This little lesbian that so many of her own kind look down on for being herself is right. I do not see angels, a human, and demons here. I see angels and a human. I see my children. Some of you fell for a time. Then, you came back. So yes, there is even hope for Satan."

One of the uppity angels asked, "What would you have us do, then?"

Yahweh replied, "Satan and the rest that are still not yet awake...they need time to see the bigger picture."

"No offense, Father," Gaap said, "but he is planning to destroy earth in the next two years, tops."

Everyone started talking at once. God spoke over them in a calm manner and yet powerful enough to silence the panic. "I have his path before him, just like everyone else's. Once he is ready to calmly speak with me, we can all move on together—in unity. Justice will reign, and wrongs will be righted. Trust in me, and there is no need for worry."

"But what can we do in the meantime?" Rahj asked.

"Oh, I have something in mind," Yahweh replied. "This meeting is adjourned for all but you four!" He pointed out Rahj, Charlie, Gaap, and Abby.

The others got up from their seats and quietly left the hill's cave. One or two of them had given Abby a smile and a wave. It was a welcoming gesture, the type you appreciate when you're somewhere new. Once it was just Yahweh in the room with the four friends, he gave them all a fond and fatherly smile. He asked, "Would you be up for a little mission back down on earth?"

The four friends looked at each other, each one grinning. Charlie and Gaap gave nods of agreement, and Rahj replied, "What's the mission?" Abby added a slight worry: "How will we keep any authorities down there from finding us and locking us up? Satan has everyone thinking that we're terrorists."

God replied, "You will not look like you. I will have an angel of mine that specializes in glamor give you some disguises to choose from. You will then go to the Elite's headquarters and reveal your true forms, and I will protect you from any harm. You will demand to speak with their king. Once he speaks with you, the cards can all be laid out on the table for my prodigal son."

"What *are* the cards?" Gaap asked.

Yahweh smiled. "I will let him and his posse redeem themselves with a simple task: They will go into the underworld, where they will find the Nephilim locked up. Tell Lucifer that he may release them after feeding *them* the ones who drank the blood and had their way with innocent children. He is to gather the pedophiles on his team and trick them into thinking that they are going on a journey to feed very rare and lost children. Once there, the very children that they think they will have their way with will eat them instead. Justice will be served."

"Hold up!" Charlie said. "So, Lucifer brings these guys to free the children of the Fallen...under the impression that they're just going to feed some kids in cages?" They all laughed at the setup to this.

"This could actually work!" Rahj remarked.

Abby nodded and said, "This *will* work!"

Gaap added, "Well, we *do* need to make sure that the word *Nephilim* is never brought up. A few of these guys will know a little bit about them, I would imagine. You can't lure someone into the mouths of giants if they know they're heading for a trap."

The four friends agreed to be very careful about what they would say to anyone other than Lucifer himself.

The sculpture-like, flawlessly beautiful winged being sat atop the gates of heaven, deep in thought. So many musical scores he had accomplished, so many ideas for new sounds, yet the freethinking that he and his angelic brethren had been gifted perplexed him. Why had his father given him the nature to be so selfish, prideful, and sometimes even envious? Why did he, Lucifer, always have to choose the path of light and righteousness? What would actually happen if he rebelled? If he did his own exploring into his own nature, what would happen? These were the thoughts that started it all.

He now sat in his favorite private office, in Vatican City, putting pressure onto his physical form's head, with his fingers, trying to nurse the headache he wasn't quite used to. That fight with

God had angered and confused him greatly. How could there still be hope for him? According to scripture, he was doomed forever! Had God said that, though, or had man? The writers of old had been *influenced* by fallen angels so that chaos and hatred would spread unchecked and corrupt humanity! So many lies were thrown into this piece of history and that news article that he barely even remembered how to tell the truth from the lies!

All he knew was he felt he had raised these humans himself, being stuck down here with them for so long. He found some to be rather fascinating. Still, others had let their dark side corrupt them so much that even he, Lucifer, wanted to throw them out into space with no suit or oxygen! Pedophiles were his least favorite. Yet there was a large group of them in his Elite's most inner circle of humans. Every so often, Lucifer took it upon himself to visit one in their sleep, posing as a crying little six-year-old boy. As the pedophile would get up all excited, most started their wicked game by putting a comforting hand on the little boy's shoulder. Some would begin with, "Aw, what's wrong, little buddy?" and others would ask, "Are you lost? Poor thing."

Lucifer would then grow and reshape his form into that of a great dragon. He would eat the pedophile in like, three chomps. He chomped down slowly, though, so as to make their suffering last a little while. He would remain in the dragon form long enough to poop them out. He would even then discard their remains into a monolith. Little did he know, Yahweh would then transport those remains to the locked-up Nephilim to feed on. Lucifer would make it seem like the pedophile in question had simply gone to Bermuda for a vacation and never come back. When another member of the Elite would ask about them, Marie would always have a similar response, such as, "Oh, Fred went scuba diving around the Bermuda Triangle and never made it back."

It was funny, really. Lucifer and God working together (not that Lucifer knew) to feed the fallen angels' imprisoned children with the actual scum of the earth. King Chaos, as Lucifer liked to call himself now, was interrupted in his deep thinking by his second-in-command coming into the room.

Marie was in a slight panic as she came hurrying in. "Am I interrupting? I hope not. There are things going on that we need to discuss."

Lucifer looked up and quietly watched Marie seat herself across from him at his marble desk.

"What now?" he asked in mild irritation.

"Well, things have been getting funny all over the place this week. There's been a global plague of locusts. Then the earthquake the other day—well, it's been one of many. There were three tsunamis! I just...I don't know what to tell the others. They've been asking me...is this signifying the end that you've been looking for?"

Lucifer snapped out of his "woe is me" funk immediately. He jumped up. Had Yahweh finally given him a sign? Lucifer pulled Marie out of her seat and led her over to his Tub of Knowledge. He said, "Show me these things. What exactly have you seen?"

This Tub of Knowledge was a large brown wooden tub of smoky gray and white clouds that rolled around in the tub. Marie had used it before, and she knew what to do. She dipped a hand into the clouds and began to stir them around. Usually, Lucifer scared her senseless. Yet he had become more quiet and reserved lately. She felt more at ease around him now. It was easier for her to rant about the wild goose chase he had them on as of late. There were things only God and other angels knew about Lucifer, but I'll get to that later.

Marie stirred these strange clouds around. Images formed within as she removed her hand from the tub. Locusts were shown hopping from car to car in traffic jams. They hopped out of people's grocery bags as the people were getting groceries out of their cars. They had even infested zoos, including one where a hippo was shown sinking deeper into the water to get a few off his backside. Streetlamps fell onto parked cars during yet another earthquake. The ground opened up and swallowed some people in a metropolitan area during one earthquake. Dead crops were shown in countless areas. Yet, a smile crossed the lips of King Chaos.

"See?" Marie commented to the greatest fallen angel. She saw the look of triumph flash across his face briefly. She asked, "So, this is good news?"

Lucifer got serious now. He looked at his main human pawn and replied, "Never mind all that. Focus on finding the traitors and that Abby girl. That is the top priority. Bring them to me...alive."

Marie was so confused at this response. She didn't argue, though. She simply bowed her head, saying to the one she felt the world needed, “Yes, Your Majesty,” She left his office feeling just as ruffled as before.

Lucifer, though…a change was starting to take hold in him. He pondered Abby’s message of hope. Could even he redeem himself in God’s eyes? Had that been the whole point of the purgatory that they’d been subjected to?

CHAPTER 10

Galaxies away, Abby and her posse prepared for their descent back to earth. They had met with a very stylish angel named Betty. That's right—there were also female angels! Betty was the definition of glamour. She sparkled and yet didn't seem to have any cosmetics upon her lovely face. Her tan was flawless. Her eyes were sassy and seemed to dance a tango of purples and oranges. Her hair was burgundy colored and went just a little past her shoulders. Her teeth were pearly white, and her smile made one feel all warm inside. Though some went around nude here (hey, it was heaven, not church), she rocked pale green attire to the nines while she souped these adventurers' appearances up to the most unrecognizable types possible.

As she fiddled with Abby's hair, she said, "Don't worry, honey. I am gonna have you looking *fabulous!* Just give me an idea of the hair style and color you're looking for, and I will have you turning heads!"

Abby replied, "But I don't want to be noticed."

Betty nodded in agreement and said, "Noted! I can work with that. You will still look gorgeous, though. That's how Betty does it!"

Abby trusted her to do just fine. She gave the lovely angel a smile and asked, "Could I get purple hair that's kind of short, but still girly? I was thinking the shade of purple like the shade most pronounced in your eyes. They look like their own universe." Abby added, "I'm sorry if that sounded flirty. You're one of the few angels whose eyes I've actually gotten to see up close."

Betty smiled. "Don't worry about it, dear. I'm one of a kind. So, you want to go for a nineties punk look then?"

Abby replied, "Wow, yes! I've never gotten to go that route! They'd never guess I'm Abby when we get back down there!"

Betty tut-tutted. "Nah ah-nah-ah. You are not Abby now! You are...Melody! Abby thought over the name and then asked the stylist, "Do you mean Melanie?"

She was shocked and inspired by Betty's reply: "No, no, you silly thing. You are Melody! You are like the tune in a song. Your personality reflects it. See, a melody can be high or low, soft or loud—as can you!"

Abby laughed with great feelings of inspiration. "Wow, I really like that! Yeah! I can do this!"

Betty smiled and replied, "Oh, I know. You humans are like different shows for us up here. You're my favorite."

Abby was very flattered to hear this. The makeover went very well for her too. Abby left Betty's chair looking like a punkish twenty-year-old who rocked the new name of Melody Diehard. She thanked Betty over and over again when shown her reflection. She was completely unrecognizable now.

Betty simply said, "Oh, dear, it's *my* pleasure!"

So Abby went to the salon's lounge for cocktails while she waited on her friends' makeovers.

Charlie was next. Getting to pose as a human, he was too excited to have an idea as to what kind of guy he wanted to act out. Betty got him comfortably situated and asked, "So, what kind of man are you? If you want to seem like you're the type that would be hanging around Abby, she is now known as Melody Diehard. She's gone with a nineties punk-girl look and persona."

Charlie had to really think it over. He said "Hmmm" a few times as he pondered this news.

Betty finally offered some ideas: "Well, I could do a cute gothic look for you, or perhaps edgy and emo."

"I really don't want to fake the gothic stuff," Charlie said.

Betty nodded. "You want to flaunt a little style now that you can, don't you? I get it. I could make you the skater-boy type. You'd just use your skateboard whenever, really. It matches your persona. You could be...Donnie! I'm thinking wavy golden-brown hair, brown eyes, and gauges in your ears. How does that sound?"

Charlie shrugged. "Sounds like fun."

This left Rahj and Gaap. Gaap was the most complicated out of the two. He was just, particular, really. He sat down in Betty's chair and sighed dramatically. He then said to heaven's best stylist, "I can't be obvious, but, ohh...if you could throw me a Vampire Lestat look, I know it fits in with Melody and Donnie."

Betty tut-tutted, and then said, "Only *Cupid* would be so extra. I can do something with that air to it. You are going with the name Tommy. You will be dark and quiet, in mood and looks—the very opposite of Gaap! You up to the challenge?"

Gaap moaned out, "Ooh, it will be my hardest role yet, alas. I can do it, though."

Betty shook her head, rolling her beautiful eyes. She made it happen, though, and Gaap got out of the stylist chair as the deep and moody Tommy.

This left Rahj. He gave Betty a pleasant smile as he sat down. She returned the smile and asked, "So, how about you, handsome?"

Rahj tried to sound confident as he replied, "I could just be a skater boy, like Charlie, really."

Betty shook her head in disagreement. She circled Rahj and said, "You need to be the *opposite* of you. The quiet, obedient, ex-legionnaire needs to be a cocky rock star wannabe—maybe you're an up-and-coming rocker even."

Rahj was nervous as he thought about breaking out of his shell. "I...umm...I, oh man." He felt lost.

Betty gave him some words of comfort. "You are perfectly capable of this, Rahj. Come on—you rebelled against God himself! That wasn't Lucifer only. That was also you, yourself...an individual: your mind, your decision, you. Rahj. You will be Theo."

Rahj realized then, for the first time, he was in charge of his own destiny! In knowing this, he let himself become Theo.

The adventurers were ready to go! Betty sent them all off to the throne room in new looks and high spirits. They gave each other their approvals, recited and memorized each others' names, and said their farewells to Yahweh. He spoke to them from a throne that looked to be part of the universe just carved into the universe for him and him alone. "I am glad to see you looking the part. Now just get into character, and get to my prodigal son." He opened his arms of light, and the room faded away.

Their setting changed to a dark alley in the middle of the night, somewhere in New York City. The sounds of car horns, talking, and music startled them. Gaap lost his balance and fell back into a trash can. It fell over onto the ground, along with him. The others laughed, but Theo helped him up. "That's how to make an entrance, buddy," he joked with his ex-commander.

Tommy (Gaap) dusted himself off in a huff. Yet he got himself into character, shrugged it off, and said, "Whatever, man. Where's the loser we're lookin' for?"

Melody shrugged and said, "Just make a monolith and think about Luce."

They got a surprise, though. Yahweh had sent them all back completely human. The angels could now only do what the average mortal could! Charlie, now Donnie, laughed, and commented, "He's made us less of a threat to Satan."

"Damn!" Theo said.

Donnie tried to form a monolith a few more times, though. He was hoping that this was simply a joke. Finally, he had to admit to himself that it was no joke. Donnie punched the wall in frustration and realized how painful that could be as a mortal.

Melody tried to calm him down. "Hey, it's okay! We're being searched for by him. So, let's just get out of this alley, walk around a little...see what happens."

Theo nodded and said, "I'm down."

The others agreed. They exited the alley and began to walk around the city together. They made it to a nearby bar with no trouble. They ordered beers and took a seat near the jukebox.

Tommy commented to the others, "I forgot that we look so different now."

Donnie nodded. "We could go to the Vatican with no problems."

They drank their beers as they let the vibes of the music relax them. Eventually, Theo said. "Okay, so we get airplane tickets to Italy after this, I'm thinking."

"We do still have money at least, so count the blessings," Melody said. She was trying to make light of the situation where the angels no longer had their powers. They clanged their beers together after she added, "Cheers, to figuring it out for ourselves."

Nobody paid them any attention here. It was a great start to utter danger, really. They had a good few beers together. They sat and drank with each other and even sang together. Overall it was a great moment for them to really get to know each other. Absolutely the best piece of information they found out was that Theo (Rahj) had always wanted a pet hamster and had been too busy serving Gaap to ever get one. It was the little things like this that one cherished.

Melody made a comment after a while about something more otherworldly. "You know, I would've never known that there are female angels too."

None of the other customers seemed to be listening, so Donnie (Charlie) replied, "Yeah, we mostly kept that one a secret; only a select few on the Left Hand Path knew that one. More humans were prone to shit all over each other's rights with the number one religion teaching that angels are only men."

Melody shook her head. "You sick fucks." They all laughed together about it, though. Melody added, "Your eyes, well, Betty's eyes...it was seriously like looking into a galaxy! I mean, is that normal for you?"

Theo explained, "We have bits of space in our sight. It's kind of complicated to explain, though."

Melody exclaimed, "That is amazing! Everyone talks about your wings, but those eyes...they are a masterpiece!"

Donnie (Gaap) reminisced, "Mine are like one of the more violet shades of our universe."

There was a quiet Mediterranean man sitting nearby who began listening to them after this remark.

Meanwhile, Lucifer was strolling down memory lane again. The visions of him and Gabriel walking together through the Phoenix Gardens came back to him. The two highest-ranking seraphim angels were arguing. Lucifer had tried to rant to Gabriel, to confide in him, really. "I just think we should try some new things," he'd told Gabriel.

But he'd received the automated response: "There is no need. We should simply stick to the basics. Good is how it is supposed to be. Why investigate something unfamiliar?"

"Why *not*?" Lucifer argued. "Don't you think that's why he gave us the ability to step to the left while everyone else is stepping to the right?"

Gabriel shook his head. "Stick to making music, my friend."

Lucifer retorted, "Why? I think we should get the full experience!"

Gabriel wouldn't go for this idea, though. He replied, "That is too deep, too dark. It is just too... out there."

Lucifer stopped walking with him. Gabriel stopped and turned to look at the angel that was given the best wings out of all of them. Lucifer commented, "You mean that it's not the norm. So?"

Gabriel gave him a swift reply before hurrying off. "It is too *different*, Lucifer. I will see you in our next choir meeting."

As Lucifer watched Gabriel leave the garden, he felt disgusted with the rule-abiding puppet. They never would see eye to eye if Gabriel was going to live eternity on autopilot.

Snapping back to the here and now, King Chaos was getting ready for a press conference where he was going to be explaining more lies for the sheeple to eat up.

As for the Mediterranean man, he was very interested in the conversation that Melody was having with the other rockers a few tables over. No humans knew about the eyes of angels. No human in the here and now had ever seen the actual eyes of one! Mara gazed at these punks in irritated wonder, through the eyes of his own mortal he was using to enjoy a few beers. Who were these mortals? The demon who specialized in temptation had to know! The more this bearded, middle-aged "man" listened, the more he noticed.

Each one of these rockers would look around every now and then, as if to make sure that they weren't being watched. Why would they need to do that? A crazy thought came to Mara. What if these were the terrorists that his king was looking for? They could be in disguise! As soon as he heard one of them bring up the Vatican in Italy, he knew that they were worth keeping an eye on. He wouldn't follow them himself, of course. He could tell that they would pick up on it. So, he texted his three best buddies out of the Fallen. They went by the names of Rati, Raga, and Tanha. They were all women. So they were less likely to be thought to be demons. He told them in a group text what was up and took a picture of the suspects. He sent them the image, unbeknownst to Melody and the others.

So it was that this Mara succeeded in giving his kind the tip-off, and our heroes had no clue whatsoever. The female closest to where they were was Tanha. She was the demon of impatience. Always in a hurry, she was much more reliable than the other two. Raga was too focused on her sexual empire, and Rati was never focused enough. Tanha was a go-getter. Even in this more digital age, she always wore a black-and-silver watch. It was just her thing, really. So she is the one who followed Melody and the angels from the bar to the airport. She followed them at a good pace and texted Raga that they seemed to definitely be heading her way. They were Vatican City bound for sure.

Tanha said to the self-centered demoness, "Sounds like a matter of some urgency. You might want to put your sex toys away for a while. I definitely don't think these punk rockers are who they appear to be." She could sense her sister scoff through the text, so she added a second message: "They spoke not of just our wings, but of our eyes too."

Miles and miles away, Raga read the second message while she sipped on a martini in her sex hammock. The shock caused her to drop the martini as she reread the message. She backed up and looked over the image of the four that Mara had originally sent. They looked completely different than the ones that King Chaos had everyone looking for. Yet wouldn't they know that a disguise was their best option right now? So, Raga replied: "I will watch them. Just let me know when they're getting here and where to go."

She went to her favorite wardrobe to find a fitting disguise of her own. She wouldn't stop there, though. Were they who Mara suspected them to be, Raga would have her best prostitutes lure them each into their own little trap. She would choose one for each that she knew they wouldn't be able to resist. Being the kind of demon that she was, she was great at sensing the sexual urges of everyone, human and angel alike. She was the absolute best at it, which is why she had such a strong sexual empire in the business world.

Poor Melody and the others...they didn't stand a chance.

The process getting there went smoothly enough. They got off the plane talking and joking with each other about anything and everything. They sat at a coffee shop to map out how to get to the Vatican. But just a table over sat Raga. She looked like a cute hipster seemingly minding her own business as she sipped on a latte looking at her laptop.

Melody was commenting to the others, "I say we Uber to Vatican City. Then, we go on foot. We can look like the average tourists, snap some pictures, and make our way to the Vatican."

Tommy sighed. "Well, we can't get there by monolith anymore."

Theo gave his old commander a pep talk. "We have to do it the hard way. Yahweh wants us to. It just means that we *can* do it, though."

Raga heard it all and threw her own seduction trap into motion. These were the ones that her king was looking for! She analyzed what each of them couldn't resist sexually, and then she put her prostitutes in place. She messaged each lady about which trap to set and which victim to go for. It would be very simple. She messaged them all right before she casually got up from her table, too, so they would time everything just right.

Even the Uber driver that picked up Melody and the others was part of Raga's trap. She was a raven-haired beauty that seemed to have her eyes on Charlie (Donnie). "My first tourists today! Welcome to Italy!" the driver greeted them. She did a double take with Donnie. She lowered her shades and looked him over. "Oh, please be single."

Her words made Donnie blush, and he muttered, "I-I am single, but I-I'm not from here."

The driver gathered herself and replied, "My apologies guys, where to?"

"We have it on the maps for you," Theo said.

The driver laughed. "Right, right! Your friend here distracted me. Vatican City?" she scoffed. "How boring! Why don't you all come and see how we live it up in Italy first? I won't charge you any extra miles. I have so many attractive friends for you all!"

How did they let themselves fall for this? Their driver was quite the Italian beauty.

Donnie urged his buddies, "We *do* deserve a break."

The driver urged them on, "You're not from here! Of course you deserve it!"

Well, there they went. They had succumbed to Raga's trap. Their driver brought them to a beautiful mansion, where she lead them through magnificent hallways decked with the best artwork, ballrooms where the music inspired one to let loose immediately, and a casino where the slot machines sounded like utter temptation. Gradually, they split up as a seductive temptress nabbed each one. Melody was led into a dungeon by a sexy pirate lass who put a chain around her neck, gave her kisses all over, and snatched her by the chained leash to keep her going down more dungeon stairs. Theo was offered the royal treatment by a fair-skinned, freckled beauty if he just followed her. Tommy was conned into chasing three gorgeous nude ladies down a hall of mirrors, and Donnie let the raven-haired driver lead him into a massive bedroom! She kissed all over him, thrust herself into him to really get the point across, and then led him to the bed.

Once Charlie lay down upon the bed, it lowered him down into a different room. In this dark and dingy room, he fell onto a seat of stone. His raven-haired beauty was not here. King Chaos was, though!

"Hello, Charlie," the devil greeted the blue-balled demon with a smile.

This was the same fate that awaited each one of our heroes. Right when Tommy caught one of the lovely nude ladies, the hall of mirrors faded away, as did the three women. The same dark room that Charlie was in with Chaos, Gaap now found himself in. Chaos laughed at the look of devastation that crossed poor Cupid's face. "Nice to see you, too, buddy!"

Rahj and Abby came falling from the room's ceiling a few seconds later. Abby looked around for her pirate lass and found herself around all these male angels instead. "Motherfucker!" she said in quite a state of irritation.

To this, Chaos laughed out, "What's *with* that foul language, Abigail?"

He beckoned them all to come and sit with him at a circular obsidian table. "Let's talk," he said casually. The four friends came and sat around this table in irritation.

Chaos addressed Abby: "Come now! Sexual pleasure is surely not what you four came back to Italy for!" He blew an orange dust at them, and their true forms were revealed. But with it, the angels' powers were restored too.

Abby sighed and then replied to Lucifer, "Okay, okay. So we bring a message to you from God."

Lucifer pounded the table in excitement, feeling his chaos reining in for a rest. "What's the message?" he asked.

Rahj spoke up. "He is ready to end things when you are. You just have to set your animosity aside and do a little something."

"What is it?" Lucifer asked.

Gaap explained God's plan: "Lead the members of your Elite that overdid their evil—the pedophiles—to feed the children down below. They just aren't to know that *they* are the food. So, you feed our children those sick rapists, and Yahweh means to even allow our Nephilim children free. It will be unity through justice, and then peace at last."

Abby watched Lucifer ponder this. He stood up after a moment, walked over to each of his kin, and gave them an intense eye-to-eye stare. Then, he approached Abby and gazed into her eyes. After a moment, he said, "I love it! Yes, yes. I accept his offer!"

They all stared at him in shock. Lucifer read their expressions and commented, "What? Did you expect me to have a temper tantrum? Come on now!" He laughed, and so the heroes did too.

Lucifer continued: "Let me bring in the one will be supplying us with these pedophiles. She is the very demoness who conned all of you here." He then bellowed out, "Raga! Come forth!"

A stunning Aphrodite-looking lady appeared before them. She bowed to Lucifer and asked, "My King, what do you wish?"

Lucifer sat back down and said, "Enough of that, come and sit with us. Things have changed."

The beautiful model sat next to him, and her eyes darted to the others seated around the table. She gazed at the traitors and asked Lucifer, "What are they doing sitting around you so freely?"

"My dear," Lucifer said, "We are going home. They don't matter. All we have to do is offer the most wretched humans to the Nephilim as food. Bring me those pedophiles in our Elite...and Marie too. They only need to think that they are going to feed some ancient and imprisoned children...without realizing that they themselves are the food."

Raga was quiet as she mulled it all over. Eventually, she spoke to her king again: "It will finally be over if we do this? We won't perish or suffer eternally?" A hope that she hadn't even thought she had caused her to glow amber. As Lucifer nodded yes, she jumped up with the first smile she'd felt in ages upon her lovely face. "I'll fetch them right away!"

Lucifer beamed at Abby, Charlie, Gaap, and Rahj. "I see you all as brave and true now. I admire that. Perhaps you could pose as the supposed food and come with us into Hades."

They all agreed, and the plan was set. Marie and Pavlov were invited to come with their king, and some others, to feed the traitors to some very rare and ancient children. Not a soul refused.

The morning in question dawned chilly and foggy. A large procession dressed all in black, and cloaked, followed Lucifer into a mountain range dotted with trees, some alive and most dead. There were thorns and skulls along the route, and an utter feeling of despair in the atmosphere. There were boulders, rats, and then bats pouring out of a dark cave. Pavlov shoved the imprisoned traitors inside this cave first. He was extra rough with Gaap, for Abaddon's memory. Torches were lit and carried by the others. Yet, Pavlov smashed Gaap into each cave wall that he could. "You don't even bleed right!" he spat out at Gaap.

But Gaap let the mortal play. The silly man had no idea what was to come. He even gave the Russian mascot a cheerful smile. This enraged Pavlov! He bashed Gaap into another wall, another still, and then another, until Lucifer finally shouted out, "Enough! Just head down the path!" Agitatedly, Pavlov obeyed.

They went down countless steps of stone, clay, and even obsidian. Abby found it getting much hotter after an hour or so. She could feel sweat pouring down her face. "How hot is it gonna get?" she asked anyone that would answer.

Raga played the part of a real sadist as she replied. "Silly mortal girl, you will be nice and crispy by the time we reach these poor starving children!" She let out a cruel laugh that many joined in with.

Abby did not like her predicament one bit. Would God let her roast alive?

They descended many more miles. Abby's poor feet were so blistered that her chance of running was obsolete. Charlie gave her an encouraging nudge, though. Abby tried to mentally block out the disgusting things that the pedophiles were speaking with each other about. She ignored the insults that Raga and Marie shot her way and tried even harder to ignore the stifling heat. Yet the heat became so unbearable after a while that she fell over. Her mouth was so dry, and she was beyond parched. "I need water," she muttered to them all.

Lucifer approached her, and spoke to her in merciless tones: "You will not get water down here, Abigail. But you may have some spit." He began to spit on her and had his cronies follow suit. "Do not stop until she gets up," he instructed them. So, as spit landed on her from all directions, Abby forced herself to get up. She let Lucifer and his minions lead her and her friends down the last few flights of steps. The very last steps led to an opening that glowed in orange and red. Farther on, howls of pain could be heard. This unsettled all but Lucifer and his angelic beings.

"What was that, sire?" Marie asked the devil in a panic.

Lucifer consoled Marie with sweet lies. "Never you fear, my dear. Those are tortured souls we will not even be going near. We are going much farther." They did too. They passed unspeakable things that had them all focusing on the ground they were walking on just to avoid seeing utter torture in action.

Still farther down, though, they found themselves unable to avoid watching a very unsettling scene: A man that looked like the Judas fellow in the Bible would cry out in utter despair. He would hang himself from a tree. He would go through the strangled last few moments and then hang limp. A few seconds later, though, he would be on the ground a few feet away. He would run to the same tree holding his rope, ready to do it all over again! Abby muttered, "That's just too deep." They moved on.

Nobody, not even Lucifer himself, knew how long it took to reach the final, blackened gate. Once they got there, though, they gazed upon the massive and closed marvel. The devil approached it and ordered, "Open up! I bring you a very just offering!" The gates parted, revealing a large light-brown-and-white-speckled sphinx! As this creature crouched down to get a better look at them all, the humans in the group backed away in fear. None of them had ever seen a real sphinx before.

The creature addressed Lucifer: "Well, well, well, look who has finally come for a visit! It's been a very long time, Luce."

The devil gave the sphinx a smile of familiarity. "I come to right the wrongs of long ago."

Marie and Lucifer's other pawns stared at him in wonder and confusion. Pavlov asked him, "What wrongs of long ago do you speak of? Is there something else I haven't been told?"

Lucifer had grown tired of this one's attitude, though. So he told the sphinx, "I bring good food for our children that have been stuck down here for far too long. To you as well, I bring a snack. This here is my Russian human, Pavlov. He should be very satisfying for you."

There was plenty of shock from the Elite now. They scattered as the sphinx gave Lucifer a nod of gratitude and then snatched Pavlov up with a great swiftness. He chomped off the cruel dictator's head with utter relish and chewed it up with great gusto. He then said to Lucifer, as he continued to munch on the dictator, "You may pass, my friend." He carried his snack off to elsewhere in this place. The way before them was now clear.

Marie sobbed as they headed down this new path. She asked Lucifer, "Why did you give Pavlov to that beast?"

"He bugged me, dear," the devil replied. "Don't make that mistake, okay? Let's continue."

A dusty and winding path lay before them, and a ways onward it lead to a few lava pits here and there. A faint sound of children singing was heard up ahead now. Lucifer congratulated his foolish minions, saying to these mortal scums, "Just up ahead we will reach our sweet, hungry children."

The excitement was sickening to Abby, who was more ready for these idiots' demise by the minute. They reached a fork in the path a little ways on, and one of the perverts asked Lucifer, "So, where are the little kiddies then?"

The master manipulator explained, "I will now lead our traitors with Raga and Marie to the left here, where we will prepare these scum to be sacrificed. The rest of you will go to the right and get the children. Bring them to us, and dinner will be served."

The procession of pedophiles all excitedly agreed. They then separated to play their parts. Lucifer's bunch went down a path that seemed to be made of human bones, where strange echoes filled Marie and Abby with despair and regret. It led to a dimly lit cavern that boasted a blue light. There was nothing in this cavern other than stalactites, stalagmites, and a few large, blackened, flat rocks. Marie looked to Lucifer and asked, "Now what? Do we just lay them all here on the ground and wait?"

Raga grinned and replied this time, "Not exactly, dear."

Meanwhile, the pedophiles that had gone down the other path were practically skipping onward to where they could hear the children singing. It was as if the children were beckoning them forward. They reached some dungeon cells and hurried on, farther in where the cells were made of bones.

"Where are you, little hungry children?" one bearded man called out, swooning.

A child sang back, "Come and find me! I'm oh so hungry. Small and lonely, oh won't you hold me?"

Then another sang out, "Where's my mommy; where's my daddy? Come and find me—please keep me company!"

The pedophiles ran all the rest of the way to where these dungeons came to an end. Yet once they got there, they stopped very suddenly. Looks of shock, alarm, and utter horror came over them. The hungry children were the size of houses! A child with one blackened eye sang out now, "Nummy yummy, yummy nummies! Won't you come and feed my tummy?"

One of the Elite backed up, saying to the others, "These children are giants!"

Others followed suit as realization kicked in that the whole thing had been a setup.

One of the Nephilim glared down at the would-be predators and thundered out, "Giants?" His voice was far less childlike now. Another one that resembled an ogre punched the ground with his fist and made it quake a little. He then glared at the pedophiles and demanded, "Food! Now!"

One of the other men called out, "It's okay, it's okay! We are here to lead you to the food!"

But one of the Nephilim jeered back at him with a menacing response: "No, no, no, mortal. *You* are the food."

The giants all were still chained at their thick ankles. Yet the sphinx from earlier now appeared.

He spoke to the Nephilim. "Yes, indeed, dearest Nephilim. They are your food! Oh, and you're free now too. Congratulations! Time-out is over!" He clapped his front paws together, and the chains fell away from the Nephilim. As the door to their dungeon cell opened, the Elite pedophiles tried to run away, but the sphinx dived down and blocked their only way out.

One of the pedophiles cried out, "This was not part of the plan, beast!"

The Nephilim children overtook them, and the sphinx chuckled and replied, "Aww, you shouldn't have bargained with the devil then. He has no use for such a blackened heart." The sphinx didn't let a single pedophile escape their fate as burgers for the giants. It was gross, to be sure. Justice isn't always pretty, though.

Meanwhile, Raga introduced Marie to the truth of her own fate. She unleashed some demon children from a sister dimension to come slice and slash at the wicked, sadistic woman, until blood dripped from her as if she were a showerhead! The demon children then collected Marie's blood in cups. They clanked the cups together with each other and then guzzled it down with satisfaction. The irony in this greatly satisfied Marie's previous sacrificial victims. All could be as it should be now.

Lucifer stood a ways off, watching old animosities die down as his fallen kin ran to their lost children in great joy—for the Nephilim came flooding into the same area now. Tears sprang to Lucifer's eyes as he saw smiles on faces that he hadn't seen smile in centuries. An ethereal hand of golden light handed him a tissue, which he took gratefully. As Lucifer wiped the tears away, Yahweh spoke from next to him: "My final prodigal son, are you ready to come home now?"

Lucifer teared up a little again, nodded, and the two of them embraced finally. Lucifer's wings shot from his newfound angelic form, and, well... they really were the most dazzling after all. Maybe we will see them for ourselves one day.

This ends my take on things.

Much love,
Knuckles

Milton Keynes UK
Ingram Content Group UK Ltd.
UKHW020707220923
429186UK00016B/923